JUDE THE LEWD

Thad Lomer

JUDE THE LEWD

JUDE THE LEWD
copyright © 2016 Thad Lomer
cover art by John Affenworth
Paperback ISBN: 978-0-9862662-1-8
Ebook ISBN: 978-0-9862662-0-1
Published November 17, 2014 in the U.S.A.
Published by Trijillium

CONTENTS

March (11th grade) 1

September (12th grade) 3

Wednesday, September 11 7

Thursday, September 12 9

Thursday, September 12 11

Friday, September 13 13

Saturday, September 14 17

Monday, September 16 23

Tuesday, September 17 27

Wednesday, September 18 39

Friday, September 20 45

Friday, October 18 49

Saturday, October 19 55

Sunday, October 20 61

Thursday, October 24   69

Friday, October 25   79

Sunday, October 27   87

Thursday, October 31   91

Friday, November 1   105

Thursday, November 21   115

Friday, November 22   119

Sunday, November 24   121

Friday, November 29   123

Sunday, December 1   129

Monday, December 2   137

Tuesday, December 3   139

Wednesday, December 4   141

Thursday, December 12   145

Sunday, December 15   151

Wednesday, December 25   153

Thursday, January 2   155

Part 2   159

Friday, January 3   163

LAMPYRIDAE   165

Tuesday, January 7   175

Thursday, January 9   177

Sunday, January 12   179

Monday, January 13   181

Tuesday, January 14   189

Thursday, January 30   193

Wednesday, February 12   197

Monday, February 17   199

Thursday, March 27   203

Friday, April 11   205

Saturday, April 12   207

Friday, May 2   213

Sunday, May 4   215

Saturday, May 24   219

Reaction   223

Abreaction   229

JUDE THE LEWD

Thad Lomer

March (11th grade)

My math teacher tells me that I've failed the test, but she's the one who has failed because she's the one who teaches math. Mrs. Desmond cannot leave the house without her thick glasses. Today, she's wearing a dark green turtleneck and a black skirt with dark stockings. Add to that a forest of split ends and graying roots and it's unbelievable that a younger man decided to marry her.

"Are you going to dress up for Pi day?" I ask her.

Her wrinkles iron themselves out. "I wear a new T-shirt for Pi day every year," she says.

"I bet you can name a bunch of Pi decimals."

"Up to the fifty-fifth decimal. My memory's not what it used to be."

"Yeah, I know what you mean. Mine isn't good either." I try to look worried. "It certainly shows on the test. Is there any kind of extra credit I can do?" I spread my legs while keeping my hands on my knee caps and lean in, because I have to look like I'm receptive to her suggestions. (And she will suggest something, because this is the most attention she's received from a student in years.)

"I try, I really do," I add. "I sit in the front row every day and I pay attention. The stuff just doesn't add up." She laughs. I knew she would.

"We can figure something out. I'd hate to see you fail the class. Have you considered a tutor?"

"If I haven't before, I am now."

Mrs. D takes her eyes from mine and looks at the empty classroom behind me. So many desks abandoned and crooked, almost knocked over in the mad rush to exit her classroom and enter a more interesting one. The closed door keeps the ticking clock audible, and I like that the ticking adds urgency to my plight. It's not until I start humming the jingle to Jeopardy that she smiles and speaks again.

"Okay, how about a retest? You're not the only one who did poorly, mind you. The ones who want a retest can take it, and then I'll average the two scores and that will be the final score. Does that sound fair?"

"Yes, thank you so much."

"You're going to study more this time, right?"

Now that I have what I want, it's time to ease off. Mrs. D feels like she's in charge, so I let her have free reign even though the power is mine. A few eager nods and an upright posture sweeten my performance. "Yes, Mrs. D, I'm going to study."

"Good."

Bad, actually. Because I'm not going to study.

September (12th grade)

Misty scarfs down chips and the crunches distract me from the kung fu flick we're watching. During freshman year, Misty's presence eased my transition to high school, but now she's outlived her usefulness. Crunching on that processed garbage, she'll never lose the ten pounds she likes to complain about. If she replaces the chips with cabbage, she might attract guys who are interested, who aren't me. Halfway through the movie, I snatch the bag from her and step on it.

"Hey! You're being Mister Grouch."

"Not really. I was just practicing my kung fu."

"Since when is stomping a kung fu move?"

"It's all part of self-defense. Come on, you know that."

Misty positions herself closer to me on the sofa and my skin crawls. When I first met her, she wasn't wearing a yellow winter hat with a poof ball on top. Last year, you wouldn't have seen a single jean jacket in her closet. Now, she's given up and it's embarrassing to be seen with her.

"I should really do my homework."

"Oh come on, you hate homework," she whines.

"Yeah, but I barely passed math last year, and I promised Mrs. D I'd do better this year."

"Fine, I'll go." She stands up and supports her leather satchel on one shoulder.

"Good. My mom doesn't like company anyway."

"You know what? You can be really mean sometimes." Her pouting is comical, and I almost want to pull her lower lip out until it rips. She gets prodded out the front door and I make sure to slam it before any last words escape her chapped mouth.

Mom yells from upstairs about the noise and I curse her out in a happy tone so she second-guesses what she hears. Too soused at this time of day to notice or care.

Doing homework is of so little importance that the idea is nearly dismissed, but I hunker down at the kitchen table and open my math textbook anyway, just for kicks. Opening the book at the center, I see the word BINOMIAL and immediately slam it shut. Mrs. D can go to hell. I can't believe I have her for the second year in a row.

Instead of doing homework, I head to my room and strip naked in front of the mirror. I flex each muscle and check for hair growth and acne. I'm still smooth and have only a few bumps, but that will change in a few years. Muscle tone is noticeable but weight is down so I'm embarrassed to enter a locker room just yet. With proper diet and stronger form, the path to Prom King brightens.

In movies, the Prom King enjoys accolades after having played on the football team, usually as Quarterback. No way in hell can I quarterback my way to Prom King, so I've settled on lacrosse. Lacrosse is a funny sport; it's not quite rugby, not quite football and not quite soccer, but somehow a bastardized blend of each. The thought of men with sticks excites me, but I still have six months to reach peak physical form. The guys in *300* sprouted muscle in less time than that. Workout regimens are never depicted in movies about the prom, so my number one priority is not homework, but to devise a regimen and follow through.

The Prom King title flirts with those who are beautiful. As I stare at my reflection, thoughts of beauty elude me. There's no point in living if I can't be beautiful. I get dressed.

Prom King is also tall, taller than me. My height's the average of my parents' height, and so I stand shy of six feet. Annoying to tell others I am five-eleven. Teenagers compare themselves constantly, and I can't lie about my height. Hopefully I have a few inches more to grow.

Boosting weight will be difficult, because of school's drain on my time. I'm way too scrawny. Food will serve me well if I can get my hands on it, but Mom pinches pennies, and she's too lazy to cook dinner. Boxed macaroni and cheese and goulash, that's all I ever get. I'll have to buy and cook my own meals for a while. I'll need a job for that.

See how my time for homework has disappeared? School imposes itself too much, and all this stupid homework demands too much time away from having a personal life. Most jobs let you leave the work at work (and provide direct monetary benefits) whereas school does not.

Nestled in a suburban enclave, my school prides itself on mediocrity. It's a giant rectangle of uninspired architecture dropped at the foot of rolling hills and rows of evergreens. To say that it disrupts its natural environment is an understatement. The recent developments in that area have pretty much wiped out all the fireflies, from what I hear.

At least a school in the Big City has had several decades of urbanization preceding its grand opening, or whatever it's called when schools open their doors to students for the first time. My school is nothing special, and if I'm not careful, I'll become a byproduct of its standards (nothing special). That's why I have to win the Prom King title this year.

Mom stumbles over something and I hear a crash next door. I walk to her door and knock, hoping she's bleeding out of her head. She might as well die, for all the good she does. Hearing her wheeze an invitation to open, I turn the knob and the door gives. There's not much to see because the lamp is what fell, but I see her on the floor, scrunched up in the corner where a wooden baseboard has been splitting from the wall for years now. We like to delude ourselves and call this our home, but it's just a rental.

"Judie, baby, can you get Mommy a bag of ice?"

"Sure you don't want a bag of pills too?"

"Don't talk to me like that, please. I love you more than anything in the world."

"It shows."

"Get me some ice and we'll go to the mall tomorrow. Just you and me." She coughs. "Don't you like the mall?"

"I did when Dad took me."

"Oh, don't start. Mommy just wants a bag of ice."

"Get your own ice, you fucking alkie." I slam the door and return to my room, where I do push-ups for two minutes. Hearing her sobs through the wall gives me the power to follow through with sit-ups.

I don't want to be weak like her.

Wednesday, September 11

In between classes, the pressure to be seen with popular students like Kristen McNicky and Connor Welbach ranks high on my priority list. Forgetting about how boring the previous class was, I hold my head up and walk alongside Kris and Connor's posse. Unlike Misty, they know how to dress, and their style doesn't draw attention to itself. They don't have to try so hard.

Misty's voice sounds like a kitten being blended as she calls my name from behind. Resisting the urge to back slap her, I turn around and smile.

"Trying to be seen with the cool kids?" she asks.

"Are you admitting that you're not cool?"

"If you're trying to be seen with them, then you're not cool either."

"Look, we only have three minutes between classes."

"And? We still have to talk about last night. You slammed the door in my face."

"Don't be silly. The door slammed itself."

"Fine, whatever." She walks away (thankfully) before she can start talking about anime. By the time she's out of sight, so is Kristen's posse.

Thursday, September 12

During my job interview, the manager only cares about my age. There are too many stains on his black uniform, but somehow his hair is neatly coiffed. The contradiction bothers me so much that I can hardly sound excited about the job. It doesn't really matter though, because he hires me on the spot. "Can you start tomorrow?"

"Yes," I say, staring at his shirt stains.

"Bring in your work permit and two forms of I.D. and we should be good to go."

Having a job will keep Misty off my back and net me some new friends. Perhaps they won't be of Connor's caliber, but an access point will suffice for now. Still, it can't be too cool to be seen working in a Drive-Thru window, because the Prom King wouldn't be caught dead in a greasy uniform. On the other hand, I guess a lot of teenagers like the money that comes with a job. It's an easy way to look more grown up.

Mom's waiting for me in the passenger seat, country radio turned up real loud, and she waves. I take the driver's seat.

I've since apologized for what I said to her yesterday, but only because I wanted to use the car today. Not that she's sober enough to realize that; the maternal instincts and estrogen must be full-steam ahead, because she yaks on and on about how proud she is to have a hard-working man in the house, a man so unlike my father.

What she doesn't know is that she will soon rot in the very stew of alcoholism and neglect that fostered my childhood. Difference is, she won't have me to depend on. Next time she breaks a lamp, she might step on it and bleed out. She should be grateful to me for giving her life meaning.

It's been two hours since I last ate, but I don't feel like eating more mashed potatoes out of a baggie, so I ask her to buy food.

"Oh no, that might be out of this month's food budget," she says.

"Not a problem. Jeff said he'd give me a discount, now that I'm hired." Emphasizing both facts–the discount and my being hired–is vital. Also, the name Jeff doesn't ring a bell, but I couldn't read the name on his greasy name tag, so Mom will know him as Jeff from now on.

"Okay, that's great," she says. "Go ahead. Pull up and order."

I order three bacon cheeseburgers with fries and a large milkshake, and Mom looks visibly worried about the total but I smile and touch her forearm, calming her nerves. If the alcohol hasn't cured her anxiety by now, at this point in her life, then she really is pathetic.

At the window, a young black girl takes Mom's plastic and swipes.

"What was the total?" Mom says.

"Twelve sixty-seven," the black girl says.

"Wasn't there a discount?"

The black girl doesn't do anything but blink. Mom turns to me and exhausts my interest with talk of there being no discount, so I tell her that Jeff just got out of work and left, leaving the staff adrift without the manager's discount code.

"Oh," Mom says, her voice dropping.

"But think of all the free food I'll get in the future."

I drop the plastic in her lap, but delicately place the milkshake and bag of cheeseburgers between our seats. Before she has a chance to return her card into its designated pocket, I floor it, screeching the old Camaro onto the main road.

Thursday, September 12

If this plan is going to work, visibility is of the utmost importance. It's not enough to be seen with the right people; I have to be seen with the right people most of the time.

Furthermore, privacy should be done away with. They don't need to know the truth, but they do need to think they know the truth. That's why I like Facebook so much. They only know what I want them to know.

Once logged in, I adjust the privacy settings so that ninety-nine percent of my profile is public. As for my fourteen photos, I keep those private. Pictures draw people in, and it's pretty much the only aspect of the site users care about. (Think: vacation photos.) My profile photos–or the desire to see them–will fetch friend requests as my popularity rises.

A few targeted requests are sent out, and I'm scarfing down my bacon cheeseburgers before I know it. My history textbook's open where a napkin should be, but the pages absorb grease and oil just fine.

Feeling full, I call Misty to apologize once again. All the best Prom Kings have a personal background that other students find admirable. Mine will be no different, once it's devised. The only real kink in the chain is Misty, whose position is so high up on the totem pole as to be lost in obscurity–but it's still a part of the totem pole.

(Yes, I said high on the totem pole. In Native American culture, the most revered spot on the totem pole is at eye-level, where the most intricate artwork is carved. I learned that by glancing at my history textbook between bites of delicious cheeseburger. For some reason, everyone messes up that expression–and when they're trying to insult someone else, no less.)

Like a loyal dog, Misty forgives me and offers to hang out.

"Not now," I say, starting to get pissed off. "I have too much homework, and I'm starting a new job tomorrow." "A new job? Where? Please do tell."

The truth feels funny coming out of my mouth, but that's what I feed her this time. I speak of a glowing interview, getting hired on the spot, a manager's discount, eight bucks an hour.

The conversation lasts longer than I'd like it to. It's nearing nine o'clock and all I can think of is that I have one bacon cheeseburger left before I have to eat mashed potatoes again.

Misty goes real quiet after I tell her it's time to hang up. She receives that information like a student whose lunch break gets interrupted by a fire drill, and I actually laugh out loud because she has nothing better to do than talk to me.

Friday, September 13

It's Friday, the last day of the first full week of school, and May seems so far away. Before English class begins, I come to the startling realization that I have yet to find a decent lunch table. The past three days' lunches have been spent sitting in the halls (but not looking like a loser because lots of kids do it). Although the cafeteria is still overcrowded, it's also burgeoning with possibilities, which means there's potential for seating arrangements to fluctuate.

Establishing my spot at the right table is critical this early in the school year, because that's most likely where I'll be all year. No more sitting on hallway floors. To nip this in the bud, I scan each of my remaining classes for potential lunch buddies. In English class, Mr. K doesn't care where anyone sits, so my eyes wander until I find fresh meat.

He's new here, I can tell, because he sits near the front and hasn't yet found his place with the other jocks who occupy the back row. Covering his hulking frame is a modest flannel shirt that might be an XL, which makes me think he played football at his previous school.

On the other hand, his jeans are well worn and there are mud stains on the lower hem, where his boots begin. His boots shoot up past the ankle and constrict his movement, keeping his feet firmly in place. In his chair, he doesn't fidget or tap his feet, but instead sits like a statue and keeps his attention forward. He might be a football player, or he might be a guy who's been raised on meat and potatoes and only aspires to be a contractor, to use his padded hands to actually create something.

Sitting next to him, I look like a rodent. The commitment to stay at that size without going overboard is admirable. Perhaps he's trained his palate to enjoy the occasional leafy meal in order to offset overindulgences. Before the class starts, I ask him if he's had lunch yet.

"Not yet," he says, "but I can't wait."

"Yeah, me too. Do you know what we're having?"

"Cheese fries and chili. It's on the lunch calendar."

A guy who checks the lunch calendar. This is almost too easy.

"I hear ya. I'll have to check that from now on."

"Good for you," he says and actually chuckles. "You could use some extra weight."

"I know, I'm working on it. I want to play on the lacrosse team, so I have a long way to go."

I ask him his name (Clint), if he's new (he is), if he has a girlfriend (he doesn't), if he plays any sports (football, every Thanksgiving, with his cousins) ... and before a full-blown conversation erupts, Mr. K adjusts his vest, stands at the podium (his classroom being the only one in the entire school with a podium) and speaks in a timid voice that's drowned out by the chatter. I don't actually hear his voice, and as his lips move I am reminded of the soliloquies we will soon read in *Hamlet*.

Finally, Mr. K shouts and everyone shuts up, but not before I convince Clint to let me sit with him during lunch. Without a doubt, he will attract students on every rung of the ladder with his affable demeanor, his stubble, his deep voice and thick neck. Clint's a social connector if I ever saw one. Clint adds me on Facebook and doesn't get caught. The rest of class runs on autopilot.

Turns out we both share the same lunch period, right after English. In line he grabs chips, a cookie, a banana and an extra milk to supplement the daily special, which turns out to be pizza and not the cheese fries Clint was expecting.

"Guess I looked at the wrong date," he says. He doesn't

seem too bright. It's a flaw that I can work with, but for now I assuage his stupidity by appealing to his stomach.

"Pizza's not a bad replacement."

"Nope, it's not. I love pizza."

"Me too." I give the cashier my code, resulting in a free lunch. Whoever said that those don't exist didn't know what they were talking about. Qualifying for financial aid is easy when your mother doesn't work.

Trays in hand, we walk to a table where a bunch of jocks are sitting. They talk and laugh with their mouths full, and I want to leave, on principle, but I can't afford to walk away now. They're all too athletic and I feel out of place. Adopting the role of eager-to-learn rookie sounds like the most effective way to earn their trust.

"Lacrosse? Better start eating," one of them says. "More than that."

"I know, I know."

"Do you even count?" another says.

"Count what?" I realize what he meant as soon as I finish speaking.

"Calories."

"Yeah. No."

"You're kinda tall. You can do it, I think. There's still time. What do you think, Clint? Think skinny Jude here can grow in six months?" Clint nods while chewing.

"Me too," he says.

"Me three," I say. The others agree—cajoling me with shoulder punches, bellowing like apes—and although they are all stereotypes, I'm happy to be on their team.

Saturday, September 14

Tonight, there won't be enough time to do homework, no matter what some teacher might say. Mother won't stop badgering me about balancing school and work, but her education stops at alcohol, so what does she know. It's my first job; I'm allowed to blow off homework after a backbreaking shift.

The Camaro will take me to work in style, and I anticipate parking next to my coworkers' clunkers, sporting steel and showing off my American pride. (It's my dad's vintage clunker. Mom won it in the divorce.) They'll most likely have foreign cars made of plastic. Once senior driving privileges are announced at school, I'll have to sign up for the class in order to solidify my stature as someone who is privileged and who doesn't have to take the bus.

The job site is no marvel—just another boring box that sprouted from the concrete sixteen years ago. It's on a busy road, and I anticipate witnessing a few accidents from my perch at the Drive-Thru window in the future, when I'm bored because I already know everything about the job.

My coworkers don't acknowledge me as I walk to the back-of-house and adjust my uniform. They are tapping computer screens, sweeping, adjusting their headsets, transferring muffins from the oven to the pass-through, breaking bills at the register. All of these activities require half a brain and not their full attention, so the least they could do is acknowledge my presence.

By the end of my first shift, they'll remember me. My first impression will be memorable, not because of first-day jitters, but just the opposite. Their brains will swell with wonder once they witness my high retention rate.

Luckily the place isn't crowded. Stress levels can be through the roof when it's crowded, I imagine, and although my retention is high, I don't need extra stress when I'm at the beginning of a learning curve that I will soon destroy.

The manager pokes his head out from behind the office door and greets me, tells me that for now I'll practice the front counter with someone watching over my shoulder. My biggest fear is that I'll be micromanaged and left with no time to dally, but I'm only here for three hours. If you're disciplined, you can do just about anything for three hours.

It's only after the manager assigns me a trainer that I am introduced to the staff. They give curt nods and some of them force a smile, but they all look at me like I should dash back to my car before it's too late. Here's a question: If they themselves weren't smart enough to land a decent job, then why should I heed their warning?

A few customers stroll in and stare at the menu board, giving me a view of their nostrils. Waiting for them to decide is almost painful. The employee standing behind me is talking about patience and how annoying customers can be. He's telling me some story of a rude customer but I'm not paying attention because I'm reading the menu screen, trying to figure out where every food choice is located.

Finally, the customer orders two hamburgers and soda and by the time I've cashed them out, I'm already bored with this new job. The clock says I have three more hours.

To keep the job fresh, I'm going to try taking pictures of customers' credit cards. "Oh, sorry, the machine's not working. Let me swipe it again." And they'll trust me to tamper with their card in whatever way is necessary, as long as there's a resulting transaction.

I'd really like to do something else besides front counter. The manager hasn't given me a headset yet, so I can't experience drama in the Drive-Thru. Whatever's happening back there, it has to be fun, because the ones wearing headsets are dashing all over the place, fetching items and pushing others aside. I want to experience that feeling of urgency; I haven't felt it in a while. Homework piles up every night, sure, but nothing about schoolwork is ever urgent.

An elderly woman enters and orders a small coffee in a mug. She picks out exact change, hands it to me and smiles. My trainer has a more pressing issue to address. He asks me if I can handle front counter and I say yes. Once he's gone, I look at the now-open drawer and consider how easy it'd be to snatch a few dollars. Registers have to be balanced every day, yes, but there's an acceptable margin of error for every food joint. I did my research. A chain like this one might be less forgiving, but an independent coffee shop wouldn't notice a few ten-dollar hits. For now, however, until a newer employee begins his first shift, I have to be exemplary. The elderly woman receives her medium coffee and the drawer receives its exact change.

And because she paid with cash, I have no credit card data. Oh well, next time.

My trainer returns and laughs about something that just happened, but I'm not listening to a word of it. His face is too pimply and he snorts when he laughs. Can't afford any road blocks or cramps in my style, even if he's from another district. I don't have to be friendly with him just because we're stuck together. Another mini emergency pops up and he's about to dash off again, but first he points to a new customer and asks if I can handle it. I say yes, of course I can.

This one's a looker, and he makes me stand up straight. Mid-to-late thirties. He is supporting his baby daughter with one hand, fidgeting at his waistline with the other. His hair's close-cropped, and a muscle tank top nicely showcases thick arms. When he turns his head to check on his daughter–whose head is resting on his shoulder–I catch a glimpse of his nipple.

"Uh, yeah, I'd like a large coffee," he says, holding eye contact. His teeth are super white and they highlight dark stubble. "And she'll want a small vanilla ice cream in a cup when she wakes up."

Weight distribution goes from my left foot to my right as I maintain composure. The computer screen–the POS–obeys my commands and shows a total lower than what he asked for, but no one's over my shoulder to correct me. When he sees the total, he squints and wrinkles his nose, but doesn't contest it. Instead, he grins from one side of his mouth and winks.

"Thanks, buddy."

"You're welcome," I say, swiping his credit card. While his head is turned away, looking for a table, I use my smart phone to snap a picture of both sides. All pertinent information captured, in case I need to see this man again.

"I'll sit down over here and wait."

"All right. Sure. It'll be ready in a minute."

The man, when he slowly bends to pull a chair out, reveals the skin of his lower back. My left knee is straight and my right knee's bent. My trainer returns at the worst possible time and asks how I handled the customer, and I blurt out that I have to use the bathroom. Yes, it is an emergency, which the dumbfounded trainer shakes his head at, but he allows me to go. One must act when the urge strikes, right? I remove my apron and power-walk to the men's bathroom. Once I'm in the stall, I drop my pants and relieve myself.

Five minutes later (or six, or ten, whatever), my hands are dried off and I decide to leave the mess on the toilet seat. Some careless fool will be caught off guard.

The employees are all giving me looks as I walk back to my station at the front counter. If they were worried, all they had to do was check on me. Instead, they probably gossiped, but I'm not bothered.

My trainer is talking about learning other stations, availability, school ... and anything to sidestep my bathroom break. If he's trying to move on to the next task, trying to forget the past, then he is a fool because he will never learn. He deserves all the insubordination coming to him. But today, nothing is really my fault because I'm new and untrained in company policy.

Before long, conflict calls. A customer in the Drive-Thru raises his voice, and my trainer runs off to resolve another issue, yet again.

What a screamer he's putting up with. The customer's complaining that he got the wrong order, and he wants to call Corporate. The man probably doesn't realize how easily orders can be mangled, and that he's lucky there aren't more people like me in this world, people who might conclude that French fries fit perfectly on the grout surrounding each and every floor tile. A dirty mystery he'll never solve.

The more you know, my trainer likes to say.

While the crew clamors around the Drive-Thru window, no doubt reveling in the drama because it will give them something to talk about until their shifts are over, I walk into the dining area. The man is sitting next to his daughter, who is sitting upright in a booster seat and smearing ice cream onto everything within her range. I use a wet rag to wash the surrounding tables so that I'm in his field of vision. Once I notice he's checking me out, I engage.

"I have a sister about that age."

"Yeah?" he says, wiping the mess from his daughter's mouth. "Just one sister?"

"Yup. Just me, my sister and my mom. Is that your daughter?"

"Yeah. Her name's Sandra." He tickles her nose. "Say hi, Sandra."

I wiggle my fingers at her.

The only other customer in the dining area stands up, tosses his trash, sets his tray above the garbage and exits.

"So you're the man of the house?" Both of his legs are now out from under the table.

"That's right," I say, looking at little Sandra. "But I miss my dad like crazy. I'd do anything to have him back."

Now he's standing, towering a fatherly distance above me. He pats me on the head and consoles me by saying there are father figures everywhere. Men like to help each other in moments of weakness.

One more swab at his daughter's creamy face before he tells her she's too dirty for a napkin. The bathroom sink is a much better place to clean up, to recharge before reentering the general public.

Until we step into the bathroom, the power lies in eye contact. He brings baby Sandra with him and I follow. I tell my trainer that this customer needs help changing his daughter's diaper, because the changing table is too wobbly.

"Go ahead," he says. I've told dumber lies before. It's not my fault he's an idiot.

"Please make it quick," he adds.

"Trust me, I'll be as fast as I can."

Although the changing table isn't really broken, baby Sandra still has to come with us. She's too young to know what she's looking at anyway.

When I reenter the workforce, my trainer commends my dedication to customer service.

"You're learning so quickly," he says.

"Well, thanks. I also have a high retention rate."

"The customer always comes first."

"He most certainly does."

Monday, September 16

Mrs. D is talking about my grades again.

The next test will be on slopes, and I don't even know which line is the y-axis. The quadrants confuse me, and forget about y=mx+b. Beyond one semester of college algebra, I don't see how this math will help me, unless I become an engineer.

Between classes, I walk with Clint and his crew. Standing next to them, I look like a skeleton. The point is that I'm with them and not alone, and we, as a group, receive favorable nods from other students who want to be part of our group. I'd like to note that my skin is the clearest of the bunch, so my chin remains upturned, whereas their chins point downward. I look better.

Sports talk bores me. I have to nod and smile and hope that no one asks me what I thought of the latest game. The only skill that matters, no matter what a teacher says, is being able to talk excitedly about that which interests others. Fool them long enough and you're in.

When they're not talking about sports, they're raving about a show called *Cambrian Lore*–a supposedly inaccurate portrayal of the Cambrian period, but who cares. Clint and I discuss the show at the beginning of English class, until Mr. K takes over and uses the show as an example of plot done well, drawing parallels between Hamlet and the show's melodrama.

The series has been running for three years already. The second episode of season four will premiere tonight, and I decide that watching television beats studying.

Lunchtime rolls around. After the lunch lady splashes a pile of beans on my Styrofoam tray, I reunite with Clint and the others at our usual table, where we continue the discussion.

"Dude, tonight's gonna be nuts," Zack says, pinching his team jacket by the collar. "Do you think Amelia Demwin will show her tits?"

"No way, not on TV at least. She's a big screen nudist," Michael Yulgov says. His buzz cut complements neither his sharp nose nor his thin neck. "What do you think, Jude?"

"It's Showtime. Anything can happen." I shrug.

"I mean, what do you think of Amelia Demwin? I would so motorboat her," Mike says. Clint chuckles and says something about having no lakes where he's from.

Eddie Fischer, whose nose is dotted with freckles, looks up at me for the fourth time since we sat down, and I maintain eye contact until he looks away. He takes a lot longer to look away than most.

"Oh, yeah. She's so hot," I say. My food is halfway gone and even though I am full, I'll have to cram the beans down and take a dump before seventh period.

Zack Eldin, a football player who does not play QB, suggests making a pass at a bimbo walking by, a bimbo that can't stash her phone while she carries her lunch tray. She's trying to text, she's trying to carry, she's trying to walk. When she draws nearer to me, I abruptly stand, causing her to drop everything but her phone.

"I'm so sorry," I say.

"Damn it!" She looks more embarrassed than upset. Her light sneakers caught some stains. Whoopsie.

Eddie Fischer takes his eyes away from me and laughs at her. Clint shakes his head and Mike smiles sheepishly. I nod in Zack's direction so that he can catch a clue, and when he does, he fumbles out of his chair to help her clean up. Assuaging her embarrassment doesn't seem to be a problem for him, because in seconds she's giggling, telling him not to look up her skirt as he wipes her sneakers with a used napkin.

With her phone still open, she asks for his number, which means that my plan has worked. The bimbo sits on Zack's leg because we don't have an extra chair. In less than a minute, we've switched from *Cambrian Lore* to gossip concerning Homecoming. Mike and Eddie simply pick at their food, unaware of who these people are, even though they've grown up in this very school district.

"It's like I don't even recognize this town anymore," Mike moans.

"Shut up. You remember Alyssa Z," Zack says.

"You remember all names with a Z in them," Eddie says.

"Guys, you are the worst people."

Clint fiddles with his phone, oblivious to our crap-fest. I fantasize about what it'd be like to move out-of-state. Start over and feign ignorance for as long as the community will allow; and when their demands exceed my interest, I'll up and move again. Right now I am jealous of Clint, because he has likely stomped on quite a few ranches already.

"Zack, aren't we friends on Facebook?" Alyssa then looks at the rest of us. "I thought we all friended each other last year."

"I'll have to check," Zack says.

I ask Alyssa if she's friends with Kristen McNicky.

"We're not talking right now. It's sad, because we used to be best friends. She called me a slut last week."

Everyone wants to say it: "Hey, that's not necessarily a bad thing." It's written all over Zack's face too, but I kick his foot to stop him. Alyssa is a female, which means that her mood changes by the minute. Next week, she and Kristen McNicky are bound to be besties.

"Well, that sucks. But hey, we can be friends, right?" I try to take Kristen's place in Alyssa's life. "Friend me on Facebook."

"Sure!"

After she adds me, the bell rings and we all head in different directions, except for Eddie, who lingers behind me for so long that I step into the girls' bathroom. I don't want people stalking me offline too.

Tuesday, September 17

Here on the fringe of my suburban community, this job site is like No Man's Land. It's close to the city, sure, but still not within walking distance to anything. I'll make the best of this evening shift. Staying optimistic helps, but I expect the worst to happen anyway.

For good measure, I reverse into my parking space, in case I have to make a getaway. Foresight wins the race that involves blindly jumping over hurdles. Right now, I'm more prepared than the peons who have parked "face first," unconcerned with the very real chance of this place getting robbed, so close to the gritty city and so far from the niceties engendered by my suburb's vanilla landscape.

My uniform is not tucked in; my hair is uncombed. Other employees are getting away with sagging pants and no hair net, so I don't see any problem in looking a little sloppy. If pressed, then the newbie excuse should keep them away.

For the second day in a row, I'm at the front counter, probably because they don't think I can handle the Drive-Thru. Fine by me.

In my downtime, I sweep everything within a fifteen-foot radius until a new customer approaches the counter. No one is looking over my shoulder, so I look at the open register and decide I can have an extra four dollars by the end of the night. That's the price they pay for hiring me.

During a lull, my coworkers skip around in the kitchen area, singing and dancing and excluding me, the new kid. Better not let me cramp their style. Better not let me see what those with seniority get to see. Even the supervisor joins the antics. But me? I've expanded beyond my sweeping radius, even though the broom doesn't catch anything in the tile grout. It looks like I'm not making any progress.

The clock says I've been here for twenty-two minutes, with three hours and thirty-eight minutes remaining. I wonder how long the crumbs have been sitting here in the grout, not being swept to a new environment. Any environment. The dumpster would be a step up, because at least there lies freedom. No one monitors the dumpsters, where the employees like to light up during these lulls.

They are looking at me, talking. Two of them are speaking to the manager, who is leaning against the wall like he owns the place. Hands in pockets. I'm trying to read their lips, but I'm distracted by the lip ring (which is against company policy).

And the other guy's jowls are much too fat for me to stay focused. Yet they yammer away like nutcrackers. Potential topics for discussion fly through my mind, just so I am not taken off guard if they approach me. Only Jeff, the manager, does.

He stands up straight, walks over to me and puts a hand on my shoulder. His name tag says James. "Did you really have sex with a customer in the bathroom?"

"Define sex.' "

"Like, sex. Anything, you know. I have two people saying they heard noises from the bathroom. You were taking a really long break."

"What, were you counting the minutes?"

"I have to. I'm the manager."

This lummox has some nerve. "Instead of worrying about my bowel movements, why don't you enforce company policy elsewhere? I see all kinds of dress code violations. It's all in the employee handbook."

He grins and looks back at the other two, the ones who ratted me out.

"I'm gonna have to let you go."

Before he can say anything else, I untie my apron and throw

it at him. How he ever became a manager is beyond me. He should have fired me yesterday, rather than waste my time today.

I hope they do get robbed, just so he can instruct the staff to walk out the back door in a single file line or whatever his version of the employee handbook says. And then take bullets to the back of the head.

My drawer could be a few extra dollars short, but overall I'm pleased with what I've taken. No huge gains, but no real loss either. For example, I didn't sweep more than was necessary, an act of conservation which has allowed me to walk out the front door with my head held high. Everyone's looking at me, I can feel it. What's especially satisfying is the smooth transition I can make from my parking spot to the main road, all because I had foresight.

□□□

Leaving that job freed up time to do homework tonight, which of course I won't do. For tomorrow's math test, my cheat sheet will be the plastic case of my calculator. I've etched in a few formulas, using pencil. Under the correct lighting, at just the right angle, the lead will show its message. In terms of homework, that's all I'm willing to do.

Mrs. D doesn't get paid enough to care, anyway.

In other classes, I can bullshit my way out of the tests more easily. And besides, the teachers go through rehearsals the day before the test, foreshadowing most of the content. The school year is still young, but that's what I'm expecting based on last year.

My phone buzzes with texts from the guys; Alyssa Zaianassey accepted my friend request. I send them personalized text messages, which is vital to building rapport. It's not like us teenagers have any attention span, so constantly reminding them that I exist is a stable strategy for now. What's trickier is to avoid gossip so early in the game. That can wait until I'm established.

My stomach growls and I realize that my eating schedule is way, way off. Juggling a social life, a work life and an intense physical routine is a real challenge. Frustrating at times, sure, but a real challenge. My priorities will always be my looks, because everyone is so shallow that they'll ogle the attractive guy regardless of his hangups. In this world, beauty is the price of admission, so I commit to eating four eggs (lots of pepper, no salt) before tackling my at-home workout.

Once my biceps ache, I literally throw in the towel and examine my reflection. I don't notice any progress, because it's too soon to tell; progress creeps up on you, which is why we look the same to ourselves in the mirror every day–why it's nice to pretend that we don't age until that grey hair sprouts. Mom used to whine about that when she tried sobering up.

Me, I've always liked keeping track. Before- and-after pics would help now, as my new body molds itself, so I turn on all the lights and snap a picture. Looking at the scale is not enough. To avoid deluding myself, I have to take progress pics in addition to watching the numbers. I create a spreadsheet, where I'll track daily calories, body fat, exercise routines ... Maybe it's risky to keep this sensitive information in one place, on my computer, but for now it's an imperative. Speaking of risk, I still have Hot Dad's credit card information saved in my phone. I haven't looked at it yet, so as much as I'd like to investigate him further–perhaps go for round two–a new text message from Clint awaits response.

He wants me to come over while Zack and the guys are at his place. Being invited last doesn't bother me in the slightest because I can always say I used the time to get ahead on my homework–make them feel unproductive so that they question their priorities.

Downstairs, Mom is sleeping on the couch. Prescription pills are on the side table, but I don't care enough to check what kind. I find a sheet of fresh computer paper, rip it in half and scribble down where I'll be. The note half goes under the pill bottle; the blank half becomes a crumpled three-pointer. So long. Before I leave, though, I need to stuff my face again. Lately my stomach has been so full, I can feel it expanding. A sign of progress. To keep it that way, a consistent eating schedule must be adhered to, so I rummage through the cabinets for breakfast bars. We're fresh out, but there are oatmeal packets. I pinch one at the corner and rip it open, dumping the raw content into my mouth. A few coughs, a few tears, a few seconds to write it down. Self-discipline and sacrifice.

Time's 6:04 and technically I'm too young to stay out past 9:00, but luckily that curfew isn't enforced very well. Doesn't matter. I can be back by 9:00. Lots else to enforce. This want-to-be Mayberry suburb of mine has accumulated enough of its own laws, rules, codes and ordinances, that the community's bound to collapse long before petting someone else's dog becomes an infraction. And then we can all stop smiling when there's nothing to smile about. Europeans are ahead of us in that regard.

□□□

I'm at Clint's a little late because I followed the rules, abided by the speed limit. Some rules are easier to break than others, and I know there are fat cops parked behind lamp posts and fire hydrants (or wherever they think they won't be seen), playing on their tablets, waiting for their radars to beep and prompt them into action while they siphon time-and-a-half pay from our taxes.

They're protecting the community, even though they only took the job so they could retire ten years earlier than the population they're supposed to protect. Sitting on a five-figure pension, some of them will have the nerve to take part-time jobs to support their premium cable subscriptions. With blurring eyesight and sagging asses, they'll rot away in retirement, where they will be forgotten.

I will not be forgotten.

The most well known of these pigs, Sheriff Roswell, is a bored old geezer who's notorious for nabbing the youngsters for petty nonsense. Sheriff Roswell is the one I think about when

I'm driving. Luckily, I managed to get here just fine without him tailing me.

Clint's place is a ranch near the rural part of our town, as I expected. The driveway's long and hosts the hand-me-down cars belonging to my new group. I use my phone to snap pictures of the license plates before walking inside, because why not. Why stop at credit cards?

His mom answers and directs me to the basement where the guys are chomping chips and chugging soda. Despite my goal to gain weight, I respect my body too much to pollute it.

Water will do; maybe it will expand the oatmeal in my stomach so that I'll have a valid reason to excuse myself in case of emergency.

"Hey," Clint says.

"Hey." I plop down on the sectional.

"Hey Jude," Mike says.

"Hey."

"Hey there, Judas," Zack shouts, and everyone laughs. I show some of my teeth but not all of them. Eddie laughs along but he hasn't greeted me yet. Really, there's nothing to laugh about because the basement is too cold and the floor is littered with crumbs that are sure to attract insects. There's no excuse for this mess in a traditional household with two loving parents.

"Hey dude," Zack says, "do you know some chick named Misty?"

"I know who she is, yes."

"She's been posting all over your wall. She's like, crazy in love with you."

As much as this bothers me, I have to adapt.

"She's been stalking me. We were best friends in middle school, and now she just won't go away. Sad, what desperate girls are willing to do."

Clint hasn't moved from his slouched, spread-eagle sitting position on the sectional, but now he glances up from his phone to speak. "She just posted again. She says she'll reveal your big secret if you keep ignoring her."

Everyone's staring at me. No one has to ask. I stare back at

Eddie and say that my dad didn't die, but that he abandoned us.

"What a bitch," Mike says. "Who does that?"

"A psycho, that's who." Zack pats me on the shoulder and quickly whispers into my ear. "Just ignore her."

"Why don't we talk about lacrosse? I've put on two pounds, I think. Getting there."

"Not bad for ten days, huh Eddie?" Zack says everything with bravado. And when he addresses you, a response tumbles out, independent of thought. "Yep. Sure. Right?" Eddie blurts.

Zack whispers into my ear again. "Eddie one time told us he can't go ten hours without jerking off. A medical condition, he says. And then he blamed jerking off for his lack of gaining weight, cause he was always napping and missing meals." Zack pulls away from me and raises his voice. "Isn't that right, Eddie?" "Right."

Everyone laughs again. With Zack in my face, I show all my teeth.

"But you're on the right track, bro. And if you get discouraged, just ask Clint here for help." Zack points toward the far end of the sectional at Clint, who is still swiping through his phone. A guy who would rather fantasize about football than play it.

"I'll be sure to ask him if I need help," I say, and the guys laugh yet again, but only because Zack laughed first. I may never understand why straight jocks find everything funny. Perhaps it's the result of increased friction in their brains when they encounter new stimuli. Every event is new to them, and so, at all times, they are either laughing or performing to compensate for the thick skulls that allow them to be jocks in the first place.

Zack asks Mike to retrieve more snacks. He does.

"And when it comes time to practice lacrosse, just ask me. There are a lot of similarities between lacrosse and football. Besides being American sports. And we can do scrimmages, drills, goal shots. Mike got injured last year because he forgot to warm up. Can't have cold blood around your muscles and bones, you know."

"I'll be sure to ask you if I need help," I say. Clint chuckles loudly at this, and so does Eddie. Zack fires back.

"Oh knock it off. We're in the second week of school and I already got Alyssa Z's number. I'm gonna close the deal this weekend. What have you three done?" After a half-second of silence, Zack says, "Thought so."

"I'm a fighter, not a lover," Eddie says.

"I bet you are," I say.

Mike returns with four cans of Sprite and a box of Fruit Roll-Ups, which I don't eat. The guys each grab a can and pop off their soda rings. Zack's sitting so close to me, I can feel some of the carbonated drink bubbles land on my cheek, and it's like being kissed by temptation but I'm strong enough to ignore the urge.

Clint chugs, Zack drinks, Mike gulps and Eddie sips through a straw.

"Dude, where'd you get that?" Clint seems offended by the straw, which is a hard plastic one that can be used until the day he dies.

"What? It's my straw."

"Well then why haven't we seen it before?"

"Because I don't bring it to school? Lots of other items in my bag."

Zack decides it's his time to butt in. "You make room for what's important."

"Please. Don't even go there with your philosophizing. It is my straw. I like it."

"You mean you like hard things in your mouth," Mike says.

Eddie, now red-cheeked, looks at me again and I turn away, observing the stone walls of the basement. The glints of sparkling minerals in the stone remind me of a time when my dad called my mom a whore for wearing silver nail polish. The thought of her removing that Adamantium-like semblance of strength with a polish remover she bought at Dollar Mart for $1.99 makes me laugh uncontrollably with the others. Eddie plucks his straw out, flicks it toward the coffee table. It hits the corner and falls to the ground.

"Great marksmanship there, Eddie." Zack's arm goes behind my head on the couch as he rests his dirty sock-laden feet on the coffee table.

"Screw you," Eddie mutters. For once, I agree with Eddie. Coffee tables are for coffee.

Zack scoffs and shakes his shaggy head. "Anyway, Jude. What're you doing for workouts? How do those look?"

I push the air in front of me and sheepishly say, "Push-ups."

Zack and Mike go back and forth about the benefits of push-ups when starting out, as if trying to sell me on the idea. "Unless you increase the intensity," Mike says with his unidentifiable accent, "you'll only build muscle endurance, and not actual muscle."

Zack nods in agreement and says, "What you really need is a gym membership."

"I don't know. Money's kind of tight."

"School gym works fine for starters," Mike suggests.

"I'll take that into consideration. I really appreciate all the help and stuff, guys."

"Hey, no problem," Clint says, looking up from his phone for a second.

"Go back to looking at BBWs, Clint." Zack wouldn't like it if someone said that to him, but the group seems to buy his digs enough to laugh at them constantly.

"I'll look at whatever I want, because it's my phone and this is my house."

"It's your parents' house," Mikey Yuley corrects.

"Wanna bet?" Clint stands up and poses like the Hulk. "Come at m, bro."

Mike runs into Clint's arms, almost affectionately, attempting to tackle the slab of scruffy meat. Eddie quickly follows suit, and Zack piles on top like a blond cherry. They wrestle each other like canines fighting over a treat or a prize, and all I can do is roll my eyes.

Their boorish behavior started to piss me off long ago, but I remind myself that this is the price to pay for Prom King.

Instead of joining the fray, however, I announce my departure, citing my slight frame.

"C'mon, every good boy breaks a bone," Mike says. His attempt at American slang is pathetic, but it makes for a solid laugh.

"Whose bone?" I ask.

"You're such a smartass, Judie boy. I didn't think about that."

"You hadn't thought about that?"

"Shut up and go home already, you dipstick."

"Fine, I will." They probably can't hear me, but I school them anyway. "Because if I get home past 9:00, then I won't be a good boy anymore, and thus no bones will have to be broken."

Truth be told, I want them all injured, preferably before a big game. Their friends and other teammates, too. When the wounded lie retching and weeping on the ground, even a weakling who might stand among them is more powerful than they, who are literally beneath him. Me.

□□□

I arrive home at 8:53 p.m. and notice that Mom is no longer on the couch. The Camaro is not in the driveway, either, so I assume that she's gone out for a movie with one of her girlfriends. If that's the case, then there should be a note telling me where to find the dinner she prepared, but of course there's no note, no food.

Not that I rely on her anyway, but her assigned role is that of a caretaker. Least she could do is the bare minimum and prepare a PB&J. I've already eaten, however, and I am resourceful, responsible–like a real adult. The curfew should be adjusted to favor me and punish her, because she does not deserve to be out after dark.

In any case, it's good to be home. I have to sketch a few formulas on my calculator case for tomorrow's math test, which I've been working very hard to pass without studying.

Lying in bed, I whip out the Texas Instrument and a mechanical pencil. It's really not fair that school demands so much of my free time. To get into a good college, I need to do extracurriculars like lacrosse, chess club or band; and to engage in any of these activities, there are costs and fees and registration forms, things that the parents are supposed to cover.

So here I am, trying to earn high marks on tests, make friends, be happy, get a job to cover extracurriculars and other maintenance. Perhaps you don't like me, or you think I am entitled. That's fine. You can call me a whiner.

But you can't say I don't work hard. I've done everything necessary to kick-start my path to success, without any help from anyone. Yes, there are some momentary lapses in judgment, but give me a break. Teenagers aren't exactly known for their decision-making abilities. Adults need not be so harsh. It's the adults who are supposed to make decisions.

Expectations, that's another topic.

By 8:59, I've covered my calculator in lead, and I'm about ready to fall asleep when I hear the front door open. Mom shouts that she picked up McDonald's, and wouldn't I like to eat with her at the table. My stomach leads me downstairs, and we volley niceties back and forth until I'm finished and urging her to let me study in my room. She does, but not before saying, "Thanks for leaving a note, sweetie. You didn't have to."

"But I did," I say, and leave her to clean up the mess.

Wednesday, September 18

Math first thing in the morning doesn't work in my favor. Normally I like to do things the moment I hear about them (barring homework), but there's nothing glamorous about first-period math tests.

I trudge through the questions and answer to the best of my ability. Mrs. D says we can earn points for problems if we show work and demonstrate the process leading to whatever answer we find. I conjure quips and quotes from previous classes and at least jot down the formulas so she knows how hard I've been trying.

Bell rings, hand it all in.

Next.

American History leaves me bored out of my mind, because the teacher is talking about Native Americans apologetically. All we need is more white guilt so that a movie about Native Americans will finally preside over all the black slave garbage that's littering the mainstream. At least change it up once in a while. Aside from this teacher's guilt trips, he makes references to the music that most comforts him. I don't even remember the name of the band. Something really, really white.

In Biology, we look through microscopes because today is lab day. We're trying to spot paramecia. This was a required course in the ninth grade, but now I'm retaking it because I didn't earn my lab credits three years ago. I was short by three credits–or something equally ridiculous– so the school forced me to retry. Criminal Justice is one of the more eye-opening periods of my day. Police procedure hasn't been used on me yet, and if I pay attention in this class, perhaps I can stay off Sheriff Roswell's radar.

Discussion of probable cause, warrants, personal rights–these prompt me to pay attention. Preventative measures and all that. Mr. K is still reciting passages from Hamlet. He's dressed in frills and a feather hat, which immediately tells me he did so as a teenager too. Adults never grow up, and the adult world is just like high school, I bet. His performances mean more to him than the papers he grades, so I work around the talking points found on Spark Notes.

Beans are served for lunch. Everyone ahead of me forgoes the slop for bags of chips and Gatorade, but government hand-out money restricts me from following suit. Either I stay within budget or pay out of pocket.

At the table, Clint and Mike are talking about the latest episode of Cambrian Lore, saying that Amelia Demwin got killed. Zack entices them with news of an even hotter chick being introduced in the next episode, but then Alyssa Z, who is sitting right next to him, punches his shoulder. Eddie stirs his beans with a plastic fork for a really long time, and then stands to leave. "Bathroom," he says, but I know he won't be back before lunch is over. The table's leftovers are put into a plastic baggie, to be eaten later.

Co-ed Gym is my favorite period of the day, because the gym teacher cares less than the other teachers, less than his own students. The boy-girl dynamic keeps my mind more active than my body, and I spend time observing everyone. It's still early in the school year, however, and I don't want to be typed as the quiet guy, so every few minutes I strike up conversation with a new person until my charm is evenly distributed.

At the very least, I don't want to be picked last for anything, but I'm sure the stereotypical fat kid wearing glasses will assume that role. I'm not worried. The cooling-off period comes right after Gym, during Study Hall. There's no reason to work during a free period.

I close my eyes and plan the rest of my evening, what phone calls I'll make, how I'll deal with Misty (whom I've been avoiding all day), what to eat for dinner. Before any of that, though, I chow down on my lunch table's leftovers, because eww, who eats leftovers from a school cafeteria? Someone who is ambitious, that's who.

Photography is ninth period, and it's a waste of time. Everyone who likes photography is stupid. Photography is by far the least exciting art form, but it's an easy elective. Point and click. Oh yeah, that's so difficult.

Just after four in the afternoon, the doorbell rings. I check my text messages to see if it's one of the guys, but no one has asked to visit. Looking through the glass pane beside the front door, I spot a purple Domo-Kun bag.

Misty has some nerve showing up unannounced, but I let her in because she contains sensitive information. What I wouldn't give to possess the supernatural powers of her favorite anime character, just so I can obliterate her.

"What's wrong with you?" I say this more loudly than planned, but the message has to sink in somehow. "You posted crazy messages all over my wall? I had to delete them and change all my settings. I was this close to deleting you altogether."

Misty stands unfazed, her glasses firm enough in place that she doesn't push the bridge up with her pinky finger. "That's right. You ignored me."

"And you didn't think of calling first?"

"You ignored me."

I consider that she may be factually correct. I now have many friends clogging up my phone with love–and she doesn't. It has to be killing her, knowing that I've moved on and that she's stuck in the realm of outcasts.

"I must have missed it."

"You must have missed it? I texted you fourteen times."

"You're such a freak. Wouldn't it be easier to call? Maybe leave a voice mail in Japanese, just for kicks?"

"You still would have ignored me." Misty crosses her arms and looks away. I sit on the couch and notice that the note I left for Mom last night is still there. The prescription pills aren't.

"I was busy picking up my mom's medication and I couldn't be on the phone while driving, you loon." I show her the handwritten note from yesterday. Even though Mom could walk through the front door at any second, I stand by my lie. By far the most exciting moment of the day, because the lie's effect gives me an edge she can't deny.

"I'm sorry," she says.

"I just have a lot to worry about. I've been sitting with the jocks because I'm trying to get into better shape."

"You don't think any of them are cute?"

"No."

"Well, I think *you're* cute."

She is shameless.

"If you really think that, then wait until you see me with more muscle. I'll have wider pectoral muscles, taller trapezius muscles, and my biceps will tear my sleeves." I strike a bodybuilder pose, which gets me a laugh.

"You're so scrawny," she says, looking me up and down. She stands up and walks toward me. "You'll have to eat everything in sight."

"Forget it, okay? Diet isn't the problem. I need a gym to really push my muscles to their limit. Can't do it all in my room."

Misty suggests using the school gym, and I explain to her how inefficient that is because of the limited hours of operation. Sharing it with so many students who need it more than I do is not something that bothers me, but I simply won't be allowed in if, say, the basketball team takes over after school.

Working out should be kept as private as possible. Being popular is about perception, so no one needs to see me struggle as I dead lift. The finished product matters most.

Then again, if I can manage to find the right people to exercise with, that'd catapult me to visible results in record time.

"You can join my mom's gym. I'll join too." Still standing in front of me, she pulls out her phone. "Let me ask her."

"I can't afford a gym like that right now. I mean, geez, the pharmacist told me that my mom's card was declined last time she went to pick up her stuff. And it's not like I can just steal cash from her purse."

"My mom will pay. Watch."

"I don't know. That would make me feel bad. I don't like owing people stuff."

"You won't owe a penny. My mom loves you to pieces."

Of course she does. I'm the only friend her daughter has, and I've convinced her mother that I'm the right influence, the one to keep her safe and sheltered and whatever else moms look for in their children's friends.

"If you really think that's a good idea, then I'm on board. Every little bit helps." I pat my chest and she gawks. Still, after all the years we've hung out, she thinks she has a chance with me. I don't want her to turn into an obsessed lunatic, so I decide to keep her close, feed her enough so that she won't investigate me further.

"Speaking of mothers, I'd better get out of here before yours comes home. I know she's not feeling well lately. I mean, that's what you told me."

"Yeah, right. You should probably get going."

"I will." Misty delights in picking up her ugly Domo-kun bag, probably because she got what she came here for. The prospect of working out with her is not an exciting one, but anything can happen. She can't go wrong with picking out gym clothes.

Then again, maybe she can.

Sixteen minutes after Misty leaves, Mom comes through the front door.

The kitchen is clean at this point, because it's something she asked me to do in passing. I can't afford to lose her just yet. Her neglectful behavior might serve me well later, and if some of my new friends can be my witnesses, that would solidify my stories. These days, it's harder than ever to discern between authenticity and lies. Luckily, I can spot authentic-sounding lies, but some physical evidence won't hurt my act.

Mom sets her leather purse down and looks around the living

room. By the look on her face, you'd think she's taking in the details for the first time. That is so perfectly understandable. Because she's been so lucid all these years. Crow's feet settle in when she squints and peers into the kitchen.

"Jude! You really did what I asked," she says too loudly.

"Of course, Mother. You're the queen of the house."

"And you're my little prince." She reaches to pinch my cheeks, but then withdraws.

"Thanks."

She sits on the couch, and I think: I really hate the females in my life. I hate them all so much more than the males, and although society might need women to further its own agenda, I don't need society.

In American History, we're going to be reading about the Salem Witch Trials. I think the Puritans had the right idea in burning those women. Mom, at least, certainly enjoys help from her magic pills. Those magic pills will doom her.

Right now, her head's not lolling too much to either side, and she's sitting upright, making eye contact and speaking clearly. She's been off the bottle for a while, so now I have to be careful.

"You look good today, Mom."

"I went to church."

"Oh yeah? Did you learn anything?"

"That I have to do better for you," she says, crossing her legs. "I want the best for you, right? You know that, right?"

"Yeah, Mom. I know that."

"You've been tremendously strong and I haven't. From now on, all that's going to change. I'm sorry for my behavior. Honey, I am truly, deeply sorry. I am going to change everything. I just love you so much." Her eyes moisten and her voice cracks. I know the waterworks are coming, so I sit next to her and hold her until my American Eagle shirt dampens.

Fickle creatures, women. One touch and they go off, whether it's a cry, a shout, a harassment threat. Mother cries, which, of the three I just mentioned, is the most overused of a woman's tactics. I have tactics, too.

Friday, September 20

Principal Snow is announcing today's pep rally–a homecoming celebration–in the gym. Seniors take precedence and are summoned from their classrooms first, before the juniors, and so on. That means Study Hall and Studio Photography will be overridden, which doesn't bother me much.

In the hallway, the seniors eagerly stomp their way to the gymnasium, where the bleachers are all pulled down. In less than a minute, I spot Clint's hulking frame and cling to him until the other guys appear. Before we can sit down, a few girls engage him and titter with a giddiness that I'd like to slap out of them, but instead I smile and even ask a few questions.

Mike punches me from behind, in the shoulder blade, and says, "C'mon, we're not gonna get the back seats if we just stand here. C'mon!"

"For once, I agree with Mike," I say.

Clint's smile dissipates as he glumly observes the back row being filled. He nods off to the girls and leads us to the top.

Before long, Zack and Eddie are sitting next to me, almost on my lap, and I feel overheated and overwhelmed. They're so muscular. They claim enough space on the bleachers to leave me with a sliver of space, enough for a coiled snake to rest comfortably. I take out a granola bar and munch on it.

Down below I see the juniors, sophomores and freshmen pooling onto the gym floor and claiming the inferior seats. There's little room for the freshmen, so they sit on the floor, adjusting their positions constantly.

Most students are looking at their phones, because they

can't all get in trouble at the same time, can they? I'm literally looking down on them and I think, yes, this is what I've been waiting for. This was worth waking up at six every morning and going through the motions for three years. Despite the stifling nature of this overcrowded gymnasium, I am happy. I waited three years to sit at the top. I am happy.

Our school mascot, the Royal Ocelot, is purple and wears a black cape. Down on the floor, it's standing next to the teachers, holding a coffee mug. The Royal Ocelot looks wimpier in person. The costume is too soft and rounded to be anything but a joke, but the banners show sharp teeth and narrow eyes.

The other schools must laugh at us, and that gives me pause in considering the lacrosse team. A glaring reminder of the uniform I'll be wearing serves as both warning and encouragement. Yes, such an ugly purple uniform is a fashion disaster by anyone's standards, but on the other hand, if this is what the cool kids embrace, then winning Prom King doesn't seem so far-fetched.

Mike leans on Clint's shoulder, pretending to sleep. Zack is texting his teammates, and Eddie's staring straight ahead, nimming so quickly that his knee might match the speed of a sewing machine.

I chew granola, scanning the crowd for Kristen McNicky, and I find her sitting in the back row nearest the exit. High-maintenance girls sit on either side of her, one of whom is the girl I met, the token half-Asian, Alyssa Zaianassey.

As they text and fix their makeup and flirt with the football team sitting below them, I can't help but call them stereotypes, which delights me because the Prom King is always a stereotype. At least I'm not being led astray.

Principal Snow flicks the microphone two times, quieting the audience. He asks for everyone's full attention, because he has an important message to share. Before any festivities are to begin, the school must share a moment of silence for the Four Angels who died in a car accident last year. They were all seniors, and the accident occurred the day after graduation, supposedly due to distracted driving.

The gymnasium hums with sadness, and the moment lasts for what feels like forever. Muffled sobs make their rounds through the crowd, and I even see Mike Yulgov swipe at his nose.

Our beloved Royal Ocelot is sitting among the teachers with its gigantic head tucked between its legs. The coffee mug has tipped over, spilling onto its black cape, and I can't tell if the Royal Ocelot is crying because it is now stained or because of the Four Angels. Either way, I can't help but laugh.

The students in my vicinity glare at me, and even Zack tells me to shush. What do they have to be sad about? If they did not suffer an accident that left them dead or paralyzed, then they have no reason to gripe. Natural selection rids the world of the weak and, by extension, the unaccomplished. The Four Angels' accomplishments must lie in the afterlife, because they certainly did not accomplish anything when they were alive.

I remember them all so distinctly, because of how average they were. Everything about those deaths is so pretty and fits neatly into a teachable agenda. Even though the four of them fit perfectly inside that Honda, and even though they all wore seat belts, text messages killed them. They were born into loving families and had their own cliques and friends and hobbies, but beyond that, I can't think of a reason for this grave ritual.

If anything, we should bemoan their lives as wasted blips on our attention spans, and go no further than that. Instead, they will be commemorated until the next tragedy, and then our memories of them will diminish as we create new rituals to rob us of time that could be spent in the classroom, learning subjects of actual importance. No, I am not happy.

The manner in which an entire school can bond over death intrigues me. During the silence, I think of how I might die. Under which conditions, in whose company and at what age. Before the silence ends, I decide that I want the most gruesome death imaginable. I want an audience to stand powerless as they bear witness.

Then they will commemorate me for years to come because

I will haunt their thoughts until a new ghost forces them to forget. Until then, I'd like to give them a real reason to cry.

Friday, October 18

Before the weekend grabs me by the neck, dismembers me and throws my limbs in five directions, I have to hit the gym with Misty, whom I've barely seen all month.

The community gym is connected to the town hall and local DMV. Due to recent property tax hikes, the building now contains an indoor pool and an indoor track, but the weightlifting area still lacks the machines I'd like to use. For instance, a pulley to work my trapezius, an oft overlooked muscle group that defines a man's appearance more than he may realize.

Misty's waiting near the entrance in a tie-dye shirt and white shorts that enhance her jiggling thighs. On the pavement next to her is a giant duffel bag with Japanese characters taped onto it. The duffel is hardly a step up from her ugly Domo-kun back pack, and I wonder what items she's brought. She doesn't look like someone who's ever worked out, not even once.

"Here's your gym card," she says, handing it to me.

"Thanks." I snatch the card from her, nearly ripping it along the perforation.

"Now you owe me ninety minutes of your time, stranger."

"Right. And you owe it to yourself to run those thundering thighs away."

"That's the rude Jude I've been missing all week," she groans.

"Yeah, yeah. Tell your mom I said thanks."

"I will."

She stamps her feet, which sends ripples through her legs.

Her legs aren't enormous, but they're too big for shorts. Or whatever. The whole outfit doesn't makes sense, because her tie-dye shirt is a long-sleeve, and she's wearing small pink sneakers that might as well light up at the heel.

"Good," I say. "Good for you."

The overweight receptionist hole-punches our membership cards and points to the stairwell leading to the fitness area below.

"This is so exciting," Misty yelps.

"Ready to feel the burn?"

"Sure am."

I slap her across the face, hard. She steps back and her face turns blood red.

"Didn't mean to hit you that hard. Here, press my water bottle to your cheek."

Misty follows my instruction without a word as she glances every which way, to make sure nobody saw what happened. Neither of us wants a witness to that one, although I'm sure someone heard. Using her embarrassment to my advantage keeps the slap even more discreet.

"Stop laughing," she says.

"I'm not."

"Yes, you are."

"I thought you wanted to feel the burn."

"Shut up," she says, her lip quivering. Turning around and making her way to the stairwell, she says, "I'm doing the elliptical."

"Good. Good for you."

Misty drops my aluminum water bottle and the clink echoes through the atrium. Two sweaty teenagers exit the girls' bathroom. A blond-haired toddler wearing a Spongebob shirt reaches for the kiddie water fountain but fails to touch the button until his guardian does the heavy lifting. The receptionist continues to stare at her computer screen, most likely playing Solitaire as if nothing happened. What's easy to forget is how quickly one can be discouraged from acting in another's interest. I stand alone in the center of the atrium, leering at the passersby until the entrance bell dings, notifying the building of a new presence. I doubt anyone cares.

I turn around to see that the new visitor is none other than Hot Dad, whose credit card information still remains unread in my phone. His tank top showcases the frame of his pectorals, the mounds of his shoulders, the veins bulging over striated muscles ...

Now it is my face that turns blood red. He saunters over to the front desk, where the rotund receptionist is grinning ear to ear (that bitch), finally ripping her eyes from the computer screen. I straighten my spine as he approaches me, because he has to see me. He has to walk past me to enter the gym. He's the first one to speak.

"Hey, little man."

"Hey."

But that's all he says. I follow him down the stairs.

"Want a repeat of last time?"

"I really can't," he says. "I gotta do my actual workout too, you know. Otherwise I'll be too tired."

"I understand."

"Last time was fun," he mumbles as we walk past an elderly couple.

"We can do it again. Why don't you give me your number?"

He turns his head enough so that I can see his angular profile and says, "I'm not so sure. Last time was a mistake, I think. Are you even legal?"

"I turn eighteen next month," I lie.

"Still, that's too risky for me. Why don't you find someone your own age?"

"Hey, how's little Sandra doing? Is she still crawling on bathroom floors unattended while you lay into some underage twink?" My voice has risen. A few stares come our way.

He grabs my wrist and says in a stern whisper, "We'll talk about this later."

"Oh, Daddy. You're not gonna spank me, are you?" I arch my lower back. "Because I'm still hurting from last time."

"We'll talk when I'm done here, so please keep your voice

down." His nostrils flare, and he looks every which way before asking if I have his number.

"No, you never gave it to me. You wanted to plow your plunder and jet, I get it. I'm not bothered, honest. But if I were you, I'd think twice about where I stick my dick. You can get into all kinds of trouble if you're not careful."

"Well, I was considering going for round two, but you're clearly crazy. Guess that's off the agenda now." He is trying so hard to regain control. He really thinks he has control.

"Please. You're the crazy one if you're walking away from all this." I rub my torso.

"Get some professional help."

"I–"

My name is shouted from behind. The voice sounds familiar, but I can't piece it together because I'm seeing red. Douchebag Dad takes a step back and grins, prompting me to turn around. Eddie Fischer and Michael Yulgov have joined the fray.

"We didn't think you'd be here," Mike says.

"When'd you join this gym?" Eddie says.

Douchebag Dad quickly whispers into my ear. "There you go. Your own age. Have fun." Then he walks toward the weight room. Knowing that we're going to run into each other again, he couldn't spout a pithy one-liner. I'd wreck him.

"Dude, what's up?" Mike puts his hands on my shoulders. "What did Bob want?"

"Who?"

"Bob. Robert Desmond. Mrs. D's husband? He was one of the chaperones for the field trip last year. He brought all the food on the last day of school." Piece of shit, rubbing it in my face. I didn't have money for the field trip. I skipped the last day of school.

Eddie looks at me with either suspicion or anticipation. With his eyes squinted like that, I can't quite tell.

"You don't remember?" Mike continues.

"No. Honestly, no." For the first time in a while, I find myself fidgeting. Wracking my nerves over nothing. See, Douchebag Dad never had control to begin with, but it was fun to make him believe that he did, because now I can rip everything from under him. "He was just asking me about my workout. Offering tips."

Eddie, shaking his head, looks me up and down from behind Mike.

I add: "He has this killer smoothie suggestion that I want to try. Kale and fish oil among other things. He told me the greener the shake is, the better. Is that what you guys drink?"

Here, at the bottom of the stairs, I have one boy trained and ready to change topics, and I have one boy who needs a thorough explanation of what to expect if he keeps sticking his nose out.

A few yards away, I have a perfectly tamed girl running on an elliptical, oblivious to her surroundings. Taming her has taken years, but at least she's at my command. Now, I can replicate the process in less time.

"You're trying to gain for tennis, right Eddie?" Eddie and Mike are tennis partners, so I appeal to that.

"That's right," Eddie says.

"Well, let's get to lifting. Let's turn ourselves into monsters."

"Right on!" Mike scampers to the weight room first, leaving Eddie behind to scowl at me. Hormones must have been cruel to him, because he's constantly angsty for some reason. Once we release some endorphins, his flimsy emotions will be more malleable. "Come on already," Mike persists.

I follow him. Eddie follows me.

Meanwhile, Misty faces forward. No headphones or televisions to distract her. To my knowledge, she hasn't turned her head since she first climbed the elliptical. Dicking around with friends keeps the pressure on. Mike leads me to the free weights and tells me that he and Eddie are here because Zack and the football team like to hog the school gym three days a week. The three of us are doing light lifts, standing side by side and watching ourselves in the full-body mirror. Eddie does bicep curls, accentuating the contrast between the whiteness of his biceps and the red freckles of his triceps.

Hot Dad Bobby, Mrs. D's husband, grunts from the lateral

machine in the far corner. He's sneaking glances at us, no doubt envious that despite his efforts, he'll never be young again. Staying out of his personal space is both fun and frantic, like a game of musical chairs. I can almost finger a hole through the tension. Hot Dad Bobby stays in his corner, we stay in ours. Even after thirty-five minutes, we are segregated, until finally, Hot Dad towels off and exits. He passes the locker rooms and ascends the stairs so that my last glimpse of him includes oval calves.

Not long after that, Eddie moans in exhaustion and Mikey brags about muscle failure. I follow their lead. Actually, I was tired long before they were, so I resumed the position of spotter.

"Wanna hit the showers?" Mike says.

"Not today," I say.

"I will," Eddie chimes in.

"Of course you will," Mikey says, "because I'm your ride home."

With that, they grab their bags and open the bathroom door, allowing the sound of running water to leak into the treadmill area. I scan the room for Misty, but she's nowhere to be found. Most likely she gave up after five minutes. I would too if I had to wake up and be her every day.

Saturday, October 19

I'm heading to Zack's today. Time to learn how to swing a stick in his backyard. His mouth-breathing football buddies are supposed to be there too. Before I can leave, Mom asks me if I want to attend service with her. She already knows what my response will be, so why does she even bother? When I decline the invitation, she pouts and says she'll be needing the car for the rest of the week; that I shouldn't grow accustomed to driving to school every day, due to positive changes that need to happen in her life.

How like her to impose her lazy lifestyle on me. As if depriving me of a vehicle will make me want to attend service any more than I already do. Real clever thinking from this one.

I text Zack and have him pick me up in his white Land Rover. Somehow getting picked up by a seventeen-year-old driving a Land Rover makes me more angry than does the prospect of attending church.

Zack likes to grip the wheel with one hand and check his phone with the other. Not that I mind, because the risk stirs up some adrenaline within me. I think of it as priming for a few lessons in lacrosse. The car smells like sweaty jock straps, so I roll down the window, letting in crisp autumn air.

"Check this," Zack says, reading a text. "Alyssa won't shut up about last night. She can't get enough of this right here." He rubs his crotch with his driving hand, letting the car swerve, but the speed limit has kept us at thirty so who cares.

"You gonna hit her up again?"

"Nah, she's just a jersey chaser. And kinda dirty. Clingy

more than anything."

"Well, hey. No one likes a clinger."

"Damn straight," he says, and turns into a subdivision. Among a smattering of off-white newly constructed homes, Zack's is white-white. Probably the only reason he drives a white Land Rover–his parents thought it'd look just swell in their driveway.

We bypass the front entrance and head for the backyard. Five of Zack's friends or teammates are passing the ball using the lacrosse sticks, as if anticipating meeting me.

They look dumb as hell, like they only play sports to keep themselves occupied. I don't know how they can run about so freely and not worry about injury. Unlike me, they don't look two steps ahead. If that's what I'll turn into once I'm ready to play Varsity, then I should question my priorities. Maybe it's better to stay under the radar and go full steam in college.

"Guys, this is Jude. He's the one who wants to play lacrosse. Believe it or not, he's already gained five pounds in just a few weeks."

"That's awesome, dude," one of them says.

"Keep it up," says another.

They're all too trusting and agreeable, as if all you have to do is fling a ball and suddenly you're one of them. Most likely not a one of them will ever make it professionally in sports, but their bodies will take them far in either the military or gay porn, after they've exhausted options such as modeling and waiting tables.

A hunk with short-cropped brown hair grabs my hand, pulls me close and slaps my back with the other. "What's going on?"

"Um." I start to mumble, just to prove that an in-between half-word or utterance is enough to show how ridiculous his greeting is. He might as well ask me, while we're standing outside, if it's raining. "I'm here to learn the basics from you guys."

He seems to like the compliment, because he turns to grin at his friends. "I like this kid. He's eager to learn."

I ask him his name, even though I already know.

"Me? Connor. You haven't heard of me?"

"Right, I knew that. I just blanked out for a second. I think your girlfriend is Kristen."

"That's her," Zack butts in.

The other guys whistle and hoot, and I feel mildly disgusted. It's not like Kristen McNicky will age well. I've seen pictures of her mother on Facebook, and they're not flattering peeks into the future. Like I said, these guys can only look one step ahead–and maybe not even that far. Such lack of foresight could work to my advantage.

"Can we just get started?" a dumb jock yells.

Another dumb jock flings a ball between us. "Pick up a stick!"

At first, they show me how to grab the stick, which I thought I could do just fine, but they insist that there's a better way to do it. Whatever. As long as I nod and smile and stroke their elephantine egos, they'll have to spill their guts.

The six of us stand in two rows of three, facing each other, passing balls back and forth until that awkward moment when no one wants to admit that they're tired of looking at their partner's face, but we all silently agree to shuffle.

Next, we work on footing. As the orange leaves crunch under our feet, I'm thankful that we're practicing now, before winter. Grey clouds keep the sun from intervening in our aim. Catching balls comes easily once I understand each player's manner of locomotion. Everyone has their own quirks, their own footing, pacing and technique. Without the sun to blind me, I make a quick study and demonstrate what I've learned to a startling degree of proficiency.

"Nice, dude," Connor Welbach says. "I think if we use the shed as a goal, you can practice scoring. What? What's up, Zack?"

"I don't know about that. My parents would kill me."

The weather decides to solve that problem for him by allowing a few rain drops to leak from the clouds. I'm tired anyway, so the distraction is convenient for us both.

"Let's go inside," I say. "I have to eat if I'm gonna turn

into a monster."

"True statement," Connor says.

The six of us abandon our sticks and balls in the yard and ascend the deck steps, slipping into the house through the sliding glass door. Zack's mom looks at us keenly. She then smiles with her shoulders raised and exits the kitchen area, back hunched. We gather around the island while Dumb Jocks #1, 2 & 3 scour for snacks.

If you take away the woman, the mother who so meekly left the kitchen to avoid embarrassing her son, these brain-dead gorillas wouldn't know where food comes from. They'd starve to death. They toss onto the granite counter top a slew of items such as ice cream, chips, dip, juice boxes, crackers, soda and grapes, and I sample a bit of everything, despite my qualms with sugar.

Outside, the rain doesn't pour hard enough for us to call off our practice session, but we do.

Inside, I'm stuck listening to them brag about the girls they've banged already, about squirting and suckling, and I want to gag. Not my idea of clean waterworks, but I try to ignore their open-mouthed chewing. I just focus on consuming enough calories to keep the evening's hunger at bay.

Once I'm finished eating some fruit and preservatives, I reintroduce the topic of Alyssa into the conversation. Zack Eldin waves his arm every which way and talks about how she's such a nasty slut. The other guys nod in agreement.

Zack's mom appears in the hallway leading to the kitchen, and, apparently having heard Zack's remarks, turns around and walks away, still a hunchback. Except this time she's not smiling.

I alert him. "Dude, your mom can hear you. You know that, right?"

"So what if she can? I'm a football player and my dad is proud of me. She should be proud too. It all comes with the territory."

"What if your sister hears you?" I tease. "You might corrupt her."

"She's way more corrupted than me," Zack says. "Right, Connor?"

"Right," Connor agrees, and opens the right side of the stainless steel fridge. He brandishes a bottle of Sam Adams and sets it on the counter. The bottle slowly sweats a ring that induces thirst, and so Connor opens it, letting the booze breathe easy.

"My goody goody sister brought that home. She drinks this shit all the time. I don't know where she gets it, but fuck me silly if she isn't already corrupted. Hey, you guys want some too?"

The three guys nod yes, because that's all they are capable of doing, and then I follow suit because I can't afford not to. Six beers down our gullets, and an empty carrier gets flattened and tossed next to the sink.

"My mom doesn't care," Zack says, taking a sip. "How do you guys like it?"

Everyone either grunts or says that it's good, and then we all go silent until I bring Alyssa back to relevance.

"I can talk to her. Make her stop texting you, I don't know. She likes me. Not like that, but she messages me on Facebook a lot."

"You can raw-dog her for all I care. Up to you." Zack and Connor high-five each other. I turn my attention to Connor.

"How's Kristen treating you? What's she like?"

Connor first brags about how tight she is; then the discussion turns more modest and he talks about how he likes the way she smells, her straight blond hair. Not once does he mention her personality, other than saying that she is "eager."

"So you really don't know anything about her, personality-wise?"

"Whoa, looks like we have a pussy defender here. Are you one of the girls, Jude? Are you like a double agent, working both sides?"

"Not at all. I'm just curious."

"Haven't you had a girlfriend yet?"

"I'm working on it. That's why I'm joining lacrosse. That's

why I'm working out."

"Once you make the team, you'll have bitches all over you. Wait and see."

"I believe you."

"I mean, really." Connor Welbach sets his Sam Adams down and leans on the island. "Football and lacrosse are great sports to play if you want to get laid. They are all-American sports. Lacrosse has even more history here than football, dating back to the Native Americans. What we just played out there? That was nothing. Those Indians played with sticks and rocks and sometimes they played on fields that ran for miles. Goal posts were tiny, and miles and miles apart."

"Astounding," is the only word I can say. Unlike Zack, Connor actually has a modicum of intelligence that stretches beyond the pursuit of pussy. I admire his ability to straddle academics and extracurriculars, but when he starts talking about the history of football, my mind wanders. At this point, my beer's half gone and the kitchen lighting seems dimmer, which reminds me that it's time to leave.

The guys scamper about, putting dishes and food away, and I notice that Zack's mom left her purse on the kitchen table. I pretend that I'm grabbing something out of my jacket, and with my back turned to the rest, I snap the purse open and retrieve a few bills, which I will use to fill up the gas tank.

Zack won't know that his mom suspects him of stealing, and his mom is his best cheerleader, so the topic will never come up.

I need a ride back, but I have to wait until Zack's finished sucking up to Quarterback Connor. He laps at Connor's every word as if Mr. QB speaks undeniable prophecy. I have to sit and wait and watch, disgusted.

All because I let my mother control me by taking the car away.

After an hour of playing Yes-man, the gang decides to split. Zack says he'll drive me home. Connor pulls me aside, rubs my head with his knuckles and says, "You're a cool bro. I like you."

Sunday, October 20

The last thing I need is for Misty to go off the deep end and betray me. Here I am, sitting on the couch while Mother's at church, and I'm worried about whether Misty will start telling people that I'm gay. Years ago, nobody would have believed her if she'd done this, but the age of social networking lends credence to her rumors as much as anyone else's. All it takes is one message, text or email, and then the fire will blaze. I send her an apology and an invitation to come over. Then I wait for a reply.

Mother's going to keep the car all day, most likely, and I don't need her hogging it when I could be driving to school. Doesn't matter that the car's an old beater, an old Camaro; what's important is that I'm seen driving to school. The students have to know that the school bus is beneath me, even if that means walking an entire mile to school every day of the year.

Still no response from Misty. I select Zack, Alyssa, Clint, Misty, Michael, Eddie, Connor and a bunch of others on my phone and send a mass text message, inviting them all to come over. No idea who'll come. There's bound to be an awkward vibe and perhaps fireworks if both Alyssa and Zack show up, but anything to stir up this boring Sunday is fine in my book.

Speaking of books, I should be studying Math and American History. Mr. K has given us a few passages from Hamlet to read, but I don't want to read those ramblings. He's a whiner, nothing more. $x=2$, nothing more. The Native Americans lost their land and died from foreign sickness, nothing more. What's there to teach? This stuff already happened. It'll happen again.

A better lesson would be to invite everyone over, some of whom won't get along, and make the best of it. That requires improvisation, a real skill that can be used anywhere. A skill that I will employ when I have to take their shitty tests. Fuck them for trying to control what I do outside of school. The weekend is mine.

Still no response from Misty or anyone else. Time to stuff myself with peanut butter on white bread, because Mother's too busy turning her life around to cook for her son.

Noontime rolls around, and still no response from Misty. She must really hate me. I lie on my back and toss my cell phone at the ceiling, to see if the motion will force a vibration out of the damn thing. A few minutes later, three people reply with No, and the rest are still no response. I'll never understand why kids my age, who live on their cell phones, refuse to reply to text messages until at least three hours have passed. Perhaps it's a popularity trick that I can use to my advantage later on. Instead of finding a piece of paper to write down this gem of a tactic, I grab the closest pen within reach and ink the message into my forearm.

I might've gained feedback if I'd made this a Facebook event, but right now I couldn't care less if anyone shows up. I couldn't care less why they'd want to or not want to. (Yeah, that's right, it's "couldn't care less." Listen to what you're saying.) They're not going to bum me out.

Looking at the ink on my arm gives me an idea. I call my dad. I say that I've forgiven him, that I want to see him again because Mommy is seeing all these new guys from church. That's the easy part.

To prepare for the hard part, I shower and change into fresh white underwear and black basketball shorts. I skip the shirt and the socks and lounge on the couch til the front door rattles.

◻◻◻

My head is trapped in an ugly frame, a frame that was purchased at a garage sale for one dollar. Its material is neither wood nor metal, but plastic with some of the laminate sheen peeled away. It's also turquoise, which might work well for a beach photograph, but the three of us stood against a red background for that family portrait. Although I insisted on white, my dad decided on red. Later I found out that a white background would have been an upgrade. Red was all we could afford. Red was standard.

My parents behind me, each with a hand on my shoulder, as if encouraging me to walk the plank. In the picture, my face is expressionless. Mom's chin is down, and my dad's smile has yellow teeth. Here we are together in this turquoise frame, wearing eclectic earth tones and conflicting expressions, but we are together.

I set the framed photograph on the lamp stand next to the couch and lie on my back, staring at the ceiling as I wait for him to barge through the front door. I clear my mind and focus on my steady heartbeat. My smooth skin feels great to the touch, but I resist temptation and stay above the waist.

Lying on my back, it's easy to pretend that a psychologist is sitting on a couch adjacent to mine, waiting for a story to seep out slowly–and mired with interruptions–so that he may claim more billable hours. Of course, that will never happen to me. Truthfully speaking, I delight in mental chaos.

When my dad raps on the front door, I perk up like a prairie dog whose nose detects smoke, whose ears detect predators. The conclusions are rash and occur all at once, but I've already prepared for the worst.

"Can I come in?" I hear him saying. I stand up and open the door halfway for him. He pushes it open the rest of the way and says thanks.

"Hi, Dad."

"Where is he?"

"He's not here right now, and neither is Mom. She's at church."

"Awfully late in life to consider getting saved."

"She says you were the wake-up call she needed to turn her life around."

My dad looks like he hasn't shaved in a week. His hair is black, like mine. Before he says anything else, he helps himself to the beer in the fridge, and I wonder if I'll turn into an addict like him. Like both of them. The bottle top pops off with a crisp sound. He smirks and looks intently at the living room, the lifestyle he lost.

"Other than being unfaithful to her husband, has she been good?"

"She's back on the bottle. The pills. I don't know anymore."

"Figures," he scoffs. "And what about you? How's school?"

"Fine." I sit upright, alert. "I have this lame photography class–"

"That's great. Say, what does this man look like?"

"He's a short fat man with brown hair and brown eyes. Basically, she wanted to be with someone who reminded her nothing of you. He goes to church, at least."

"Was that a criticism?" My dad rarely blinks, especially when he's defending himself. I look down and see that my right heel won't stop tapping the carpet. My dad approaches me and I can smell rank alcohol on his breath. He's been drinking all morning, but of course he's a talented actor, so I can't say exactly how much he's had. He might unhinge more than he did last time.

"No, it wasn't a criticism. I was just saying."

"Well, at least my boy's not criticizing me. He was just saying." He's towering over me now, as if I'm the one who's done something wrong.

"Dad, maybe you should slow down with that bottle. You're not even supposed to be here."

"Sounds like the son is giving the father advice." He holds the bottle by its neck and chugs, and then the slurring starts. "Now why don't you tell me, in what world does that sound right?"

There are eleven worlds that I can list off the top of my head, but I hold my tongue and let him have his way. He's already started, and trying to stop him now will hurt us both more than we can handle. Tomorrow, I won't be able to lean against the backs of desk chairs, which might force me to actually pay attention. Now, I'm just paying my dues. When I set goals, I achieve them. I'm taking the Camaro to school tomorrow no matter what.

"Why don't you tell me?" Veins in his neck. He's straining.

"Dad, I'm sorry. I didn't mean it." My voice trembles, not because I want to cry but because it's been getting deeper lately and I don't want it to crack. Not in front of him. "I'm sorry, Dad."

He pulls me up from the couch by my arm and then squeezes my biceps really, really tight. "On top of that, you lied to me. I saw your midterm report card on the kitchen table. An F in math? And Cs and Ds in everything else? Hey, look at me." Using one hand, he cups my chin and squeezes so hard that I'm afraid he will pierce my cheeks. My lips scrunched together, I look into his eyes. "You lied to me about school. You lied, you lied. You lied."

One slap across the face. Tears well up before I hit the floor. This is the game I always play with him. He doesn't see any tears until he's gone too far, and as I've aged, he's had to wait longer and longer to achieve the same results. The cold floor makes my belly prickle with goosebumps.

In my peripheral view, a raised boot.

My muscles tense. He kicks. Dirt and gravel on my skin, and it's not long before he's wiggling me with one leg. Can't even bend down and hit me properly. Oh, he's swiping a crushed cigarette butt off his boot. There it is now, on the floor with me.

"I told you about lying," he yells. "I told you again and again. Get up. Now."

I wobble to my feet, trying to gauge whether any of my ribs are broken. Can't really blame him for wanting to punish me. It's a father's job to set his boy straight. He knows his role and I know mine. Mom's the last one to catch a clue, which is why she resorts to the wimpiest form of drug abuse–those pills. Capsules. At least my dad has his Scotch.

He screams something unintelligible at me, sending a few

flecks of spit along for the ride. "Your mom wants to take my fuckin money. And my car. Raise you to be a little shit like her. You don't know how hard I work. You don't fucking know." Finally, he's using his hands, keeping the blows below the collar bone, where the bruises won't be seen. "WIC and food stamps and she still fucks it all up."

A blow to the stomach, like he's a goddamn street fighter trying his uppercut. I wheeze, cringe and fall back on the crusty couch. The cushion has been displaced, revealing potato chips and spare change. My dad will comment on the mess and blame me, and Mom will be so sorry she took the car.

"And I just worked ten days straight!" His high-pitched, whining voice hurts my ears and tells me that he'll go into overdrive pretty soon. My muscles tense again, in anticipation of impact, but then I give it all up. Better to relax now. Steady practiced breathing, or I'll break.

Blood rushes to my head when he smarts me with his belt. I fall against the side table, knocking over the lamp and our plastic-framed family portrait. That beachy, turquoise frame. A real family visits a beach together, usually when the kids are still young. Our family, instead of going to the beach, has enjoyed trips to the hospital, to the police station, to the Salvation Army. Beaches are too hot. Break a gas line, cause a leak–start your own heat. Allow the hunky fireman to whisk you away after being locked up all night.

Once my father's had his fill, he sits down and watches me with a snarled lip. The October sun illuminates one side of his face from behind window blinds. Not once does he let go of the belt.

"Stop crying," he commands.

Sniffles escape me, and once the first tear drops, the rest have to gush.

"Why are you doing this to me, Dad?"

"Stop crying."

"You're not even supposed to be here."

"Stop crying, or I'm gonna beat the hell out of you."

The lock on the front door turns, and Mom walks in carrying

a pamphlet and keys in one hand; in the crook of her other arm, a bag of groceries. Mac & cheese, most likely.

Wearing sunglasses and a church dress, she actually looks like a member of society–that is, until she notices who's in the room. My dad stands up and slams the door behind her, cutting off the sunlight before she can escape. Her cheery disposition sinks at the resurgence of blacked-out memories.

"Whose car is that? That's your car?"

"Yes, that's my car. Not your car. Mine."

"Get out of here now," she screams. Then she looks at my quivering body. Am I bleeding? I don't know, but her face says yes. "Baby, what did he do to you? Jude, honey?"

"Mom," I croak.

"Taught him a lesson, cause he ain't learning in school. Have you seen his report card?"

"You're breaking the restraining order. I'm calling the police."

She reaches into her bag for her smart phone (yet somehow she can't buy a new car for me to drive). My dad grabs her. She screams. He muffles her as she cries for help, her voice faintly seeping through his fingers.

There's nothing to do but watch and wait until the neighbors deign the noise loud enough to warrant a 9-1-1 call. With our history, the police will come knocking in fifteen minutes.

Before they arrive, however, I see Misty through the front window. The stupid bitch had the nerve to show up without an RSVP.

Thursday, October 24

Connor Welbach has joined us for lunch today. Judging by his muscles, he must eat lean white meat all the time, but today he's not. I resist the temptation to laugh at his eating apple sauce, because doing so makes him look like a frail retirement home veteran.

Zack, Mike and Eddie are here too, but not Clint.

"Where is he?" I say.

"Hanging out with some ugly chick," Mike says. "You know Misty, that anime nerd?"

"Are they dating or something?"

"Looks like it," Zack says with a groan. "See, even Clint's getting laid. When is it your turn, Eddie?"

"When you stop pestering me, I'll find someone. Until then, I'm holding out just to spite you."

Eddie's sitting close to me. Our knees are touching, but I don't push him away. If he and Mike can shower together, then jean-to-jean contact between Eddie and me is nothing. Sweatpants would be softer against my bruises. I should be wearing sweatpants.

"Does anyone know anything about this Misty chick?" Mike says.

"I hear she sleeps with a life-sized pillow," says Connor. "You know the ones with the cartoon characters on them? Not the kiddie ones with a bunch of cartoon characters, but it's like a life-sized doll—except it's a pillow."

Figures. Clint and Misty would suck face. They both have one degree of separation through me, meaning that my secret's probably out. Slapping her in public might have sped this process along.

Clint, on the other hand, has such a diverse group of friends outside of our table, I'm not surprised he's found his way to being an Otaku. Then again, he's the kind of guy who wets his toothbrush with hot water. They'll be happy and fat together.

Alyssa walks toward our table carrying a lunch tray that I fear she may dump on Zack's head, but she doesn't. Instead, she says hello to the table, and then winks at me before sitting with Kristen's posse.

"Please excuse me, guys," I say and head over to that table.

Kristen is sitting nearest the window, where she enjoys a full view of the cafeteria. Although the other girls are eating, Kristen's tray contains untouched potato salad, and it's really hard to remember why I approached this table when I look at her sitting with her hands folded, her eyes closed.

"Hi." Alyssa breaks the spell from where she sits under my nose. "Can I help you?"

"Yeah. What was that for?"

"The wink?"

"Yeah."

"Because I know."

"Know what?"

"Your secret." The girls sitting on either side of her giggle and face me. Kristen finally opens her eyes and takes a bite of her potato salad.

"What secret?"

"You know," she whispers. "Gay."

Not sure if I should be happy that my instincts were correct, or upset at having been discovered. Either way, I don't regret slapping Misty. I should have slapped harder.

"You know, you're kind of cute," Alyssa continues. She whispers something to the girl sitting next to her, and then redirects her attention to me. "Wanna come to my place tonight? Please?"

"Why?"

"Just because. I want to feel you out."

"Where do you live?"

"Don't worry about that. I'll have someone pick you up. Just be ready at five, and bring an open-minded attitude."

This isn't how I expected to get my foot in the door of Kristen's world. Ideally, I'd have approached Kristen through Connor, but life throws curve balls. "I'll be ready," I say.

Behind me, the guys are laughing.

□□□

A black Mercedes pulls into the driveway at exactly five o'clock. The driver doesn't beep the horn or step outside the car. He simply lets the car idle until I'm out of the house.

The car ride takes longer than I expected, and I wonder if we're leaving the county. The leather interior of this car is of higher quality than that of the couch at home. Lots of things are of higher quality than anything I own.

I look out the window and see it getting dark outside.

By the time the mustached driver has announced our arrival, I can't tell where we are. Trees surround us and I can't see pavement through the rear window. A loud metallic creaking sends vibrations through the car, and I mistakenly assume that to be the car's massage function.

I follow the headlights and notice black bars ahead. The front gate.

The driver shifts the car into first and pulls us forward for a full twenty seconds before parking in a circular driveway. Alyssa Zaianassey lives in a mansion, perhaps the most expensive residential real estate in town. The driver doesn't open my door, but says, "We're here."

Whatever got up his butt, it must be wretched; drivers on TV always open the door for others.

At the top of the wide cobblestone steps, I see pink flowers and vines that have clung to the archway above double doors. Alyssa answers the door without my having to knock.

"Hey, good to see you."

"Jesus Christ. I've lived here my whole life and I didn't know this was here."

"My parents are super private."

"And rich, I take it."

"Not really. In my home country, we're considered middle class."

"Where the hell are you from again?"

"Singapore, doll." She sticks her hand out for me to kiss. I'm not that kind of gay, so I leave her hanging until she retracts. "Fine. Be that way."

"Is your dad a banker or something?"

"He works in finance, or something. He has a normal job, just like most people. But don't bring that up around him. He's very embarrassed to have a job."

"Yeah, jobs suck." Damn, I have to contact Hot Dad again. On my to-do list that task goes.

"So let's go to my room," she says, perking up.

We pass a Filipina maid on our way to the grand staircase, which doesn't face the front door. Alyssa says that that would be bad Fung Shui. Her bedroom encompasses the entire upstairs of the west wing. We step inside and she directs me to her king-sized bed.

"Why didn't you tell me you were gay?"

"You never asked. And I don't know you that well, but that's about to change now, isn't it."

Alyssa laughs. "How do you know you're really gay? Have you tried making out with a girl?"

"I can see where this is going."

"Oh come on." She closes her bedroom door and pulls down her spaghetti straps, letting her breasts out. "Give them a squeeze. I bet you'll enjoy the sensation, even if it doesn't get you aroused."

I poke one breast and play with her nipple for a second. I've never seen breasts in person. Hers aren't bad, but if she keeps acting like a slut, they'll droop soon. Heard that somewhere before, but I don't know where. She has to slap my hands away to indicate that I've been touching them for too long, and I think, Zack's gonna love this when he hears.

"You like?"

"You have nice breasts."

"Thank you," She flips her silky hair back and ties it into a pony tail.

We talk about school, about our families. She digs really deep, and I guess I'm honest for the most part. She's really easy to talk to. I examine her facial tics, hoping to adopt a similar personality someday, depending on the situation.

"And what are you doing for Halloween?"

"Shit, I forgot."

"Well, Zack's hosting a Halloween party. And he's inviting me!"

"Cool."

"And yes, it's on the thirty-first. Find a costume and join, because it's going to be a sexy party. All the hot guys and jocks will be there, doing naked runs most likely. Lots of crazy stuff will happen."

"I can hardly wait."

"But you need to buy a sexy costume first. I noticed that you put on a few pounds of muscle. It's definitely noticeable."

"Thank you."

"You're welcome," she says, putting a finger on her chin as if deep in thought. "Matter of fact, why don't you take off your clothes?"

"My clothes?"

"Yeah, your clothes."

"All of them?" "What do you think?"

"Well, I guess." I don't want to show her any bruises, but she now knows enough of my history for that to be acceptable. A few pity points wouldn't hurt, either.

"It's only fair, because I let you touch me."

I shrug and strip; so does she. We stand in front of the full-length mirror together, examining our bodies.

"You have some low hangers there."

"Thanks." I don't know if she's complimenting me or not. Or if her comment on my balls is to detract from my penis size. I don't know if mine is big by her standards. Probably not. In any case, she's completely ignoring my bruises, and suddenly

I fear that she's only befriending me because she thinks I'm a charity case. Like, she expected to see these bruises, and she wanted to cover up her knowledge with whimsical curiosity. Either way, I'm not ashamed.

"Say, you have to show this hot body off at Zack's party. Any idea what kind of costume you want to wear?"

My balls want to retreat inside me, that's how cold it is. "I don't want to be naked, that's for sure."

"Well, duh."

"I'll go as Satan." The answer slips out without a second thought.

"Satan," she ponders, and then folds her hands together. "I like it."

□□□

Solace at home. No matter how comfortable the Zaianassey mansion was, nothing beats the comforts of home.

Kidding. This place blows.

There's no time to look at homework or take a shower, because I've been a good boy, arriving before the 9:00 curfew.

First thing's first: I check online retailers for a Satan costume.

One web page advertises a black mesh shirt, which I imagine will do wonders to cover up any bruises I still have by then. (These bruises were worth the driving privileges. With Mom back on the bottle, I have unrestricted mobility.)

On another site I find a black Speedo that will show off my legs. And then I visit a Halloween costume site for Satan's horns, cape and pitchfork. A well-chosen ensemble, by anyone's standards. I'll credit this good taste to my personality, not my sexuality. If I've already been outed, I might as well dress sharply. I wouldn't want to misrepresent the gays.

Once I have all the shopping cart pages open in separate tabs, I search my phone for the picture of Hot Dad's credit card information, scrolling past pictures of license plates, my bruises, my dad's modified restraining order ... and there it is, the numbers clear as day. The name's hard to read, but I remember the guys telling me it's Bobby Desmond, Mrs. D's husband. I enter Robert Desmond under the heading that reads NAME ON CARD, then the expiration date, the credit card number and the CV2.

The shipping address has to be mine, but even if he reports fraudulent activity and the police come knocking, I have leverage. I am, shall we say, less experienced, which in this particular scenario will play to my advantage. He can't cop a complaint, period, unless he wants his computer seized and harvested for kiddie porn. They'll take his pretty daughter away too. Baby Sandra would be better off in an orphanage.

For each purchase, I select One-Day Premium Shipping. Grand Total: $187.70.

For the first time since Sunday, when my dad beat me for no justifiable reason, I feel something. Emotionally, I mean. Shopper's high. I decide, why the hell not, let's give this Cambrian Lore thing a shot while Hot Dad's credit card information is pulled up. There are many luxuries poor people don't have, but the cable box isn't one of them. This is something I could easily pirate from a torrent site, but considering the way Hot Dad treated me at the gym, I'd rather use his money.

A quick Internet search leads me to the subscription form. It's a premium channel. I already knew that. The screen prompts me along its script of service options, which eventually leads me back to the cable company's website.

I enter the details for each field, still using my address (because why not?), and in ten minutes, I'm subscribed. Luckily, a marathon is playing right now.

ㅁㅁㅁ

Cambrian Lore is a unique little show. It reminds me of *Are You Afraid of the Dark*, a show I watched as a child. In the same fashion, its characters–all in the titular prehistoric age–sit around a bonfire and tell stories of conquests, travels and disputes.

Each story fills an entire episode, and they seem rather disjointed if you watch just one or two, but the clever thing about them is that once they're all thrown together in sequence, you notice that they are interwoven. It's a series of stories within a series of stories. It has potential to be a bland melodrama, but for now its outlandish historical inaccuracies are charming.

Of course, one element that is consistent in each of the stories is sex–to retain male viewership. Plenty of Cambrian women disrobe and display supple bodies that haven't suffered the elements of the environment they dwell in, but viewers are supposed to overlook that because, hey, it's television.

Men, on the other hand, generally talk about violence, whether it's the killing of a saber tooth, the poaching of a boar or an elephant, the awe of fireflies and so on. What's interesting in each of their stories is the dynamics between the men who hunt and the boys who stay behind, or what happens when a boy ventures with his father and is devoured in the most gruesome fashion.

They are all too uncivilized to have civilized discussion, and that's where the real charm kicks in.

The pacing skates along until the season finale which takes place just before an ice age. Wooly mammoths won't survive, I'm sure. I can't believe a television show has gripped me so completely.

Another aspect that I enjoy is that there is equal nudity from both men and women. And I mean full-frontal nudity, not just ass cheeks. Their parts are shown casually as they sit on rocks around the campfire. As they jump through thickets and climb trees. Finally, a bit of realism. If straight men are made uncomfortable by having to watch man parts on their favorite show, then tough. How do they think women have felt since, I don't know, forever?

Now if that equality in nudity is demonstrated at Zack Eldin's Halloween party, we'll be in business. My cell phone's ready to snap a few nudes, discreetly, and maybe send them anonymously to web services that don't mind the sources of their submissions. Easy way to make cash, but not something people normally look into. Also, it could lead to a lot of embarrassment, if only I could get a face along with the dick.

Breasts are fair game too. I don't discriminate, unlike movies and television.

But now I'm nodding off and have to sleep before another day of long classes. A final test on Hamlet, a quiz on sepia toning, a new gym unit. Too many changes and revelations and details to keep up with. I should just write everything down.

That's why writing was invented, right? To remember. Even the Cambrian people understood that.

□□□

Another math test looms in the near future. I can't be bothered to study, which means I'll probably fail the class. There's nothing I can do about it now. The teacher should reconsider her teaching career, because her lessons don't stick. If she can't get non-Asians interested in math, then she has no right to teach. Her assignments require too much alone time. In other classes, we can do group projects, but there's nothing like that for math. Instead, rote memorization is the answer to everything. She wants us to solve dozens of similar problems until our eyes bleed. Speaking in a monotone voice doesn't help, either. Whether she's aware of her husband's sexuality or not, she really ought to teach better.

I'll be the one to let her know about herself.

So the math textbook stays in my backpack, as it does every single goddamn night, and I sleep for a few hours before I have to wake up and drive the Camaro I fought so hard for. Because my priorities are in order, my goals, needs and emotional fulfillment come before any math test. Or English, for that matter. Mr. K can go fuck himself.

Friday, October 25

Apparently my priorities were wrong. The guidance counselor, as mandated by this particular school (and no others in the county), is calling in seniors one by one and discussing future plans, which basically means they're promoting college.

I've already neglected several of the student college workshops and career fora, because those recruiters are more like poachers, killing the dreams of the young and uninvolved, using slimy catch phrases and decades of experience to turn students into government-sanctioned drones, just like them.

I'm not expecting much from this ploy, but I can use this meeting to hone my acting skills. I've been slipping lately.

The guidance counselor is in his forties, bald and fat, as you'd expect. He's asking me why I haven't taken the ACT yet. I ask him if he's seen my math scores, and he says he has. Then he looks at me like he's waiting for a confession, and I have the urge to strangle him with his own tie. Of course I know how I'm doing in Math. That's why I haven't taken the ACT.

SATs I took, but scored below average in every category except writing. Reading comprehension–as low as my Math scores. Oh well.

The excuse I give him for not having taken the ACT is that I am not financially able, that Mother is a sniveling cunt who can't put the bottle down; who can't pause her game of Candy Crush long enough to help me; who likes to sleep all day instead of look for a job. It's tiring.

The guidance counselor reminds me that the exam fee can

be waived for students in need of financial assistance. For those who have the merit but not the means.

Bullshit. I've seen how few students actually dodge those payments. It's just another way for the education board, or the state board–or whoever–to use the promise of a bright future as an expedient to profit. They'll do everything short of blowing you to convince you that college is worth the expense, and then you'll pay student loans for the rest of your life. I don't know how they can do that to high schoolers, year after year. Anyway, that's their conscience at stake, not mine.

I say, I couldn't possibly pass the ACT. You know that.

You won't know until you try, he says.

I stare at him. The silence makes him sigh, and then he looks at his computer screen because he can't maintain eye contact. I have that advantage over him. He faces me again, and then looks at the computer screen again. He encourages me to take the test one more time, saying it's not too late to get into a good college. Sure, it's never too late. It's never too late to join a Ponzi scheme, either. College is a scam in the same way that religion is a scam. They are both institutions that are profit-driven, no matter what some board member or trustee or politician says. They don't know the needs of students, of young people–only their own needs, their own pockets.

Screw them all. If a bald guidance counselor can't even look me in the eye while he sells a college education, then that should tell you something. He doesn't believe in it either. The system is so screwed up, I might as well avoid it. The fact that my poor performance is remotely acceptable by college standards is proof that the system blows. I can get accepted to any mediocre school, no matter how low my GPA, as long as Mom co-signs.

Actually, that sounds like a good idea. Getting Mom to co-sign on the loans right before I flunk out would be amusing. I'll matriculate and then drop out in the fourth year. Then the financial ruin would keep her awake all night, and she'd stop sleeping in all day, maybe get a job. Or kill herself, whichever comes first. Either way, I'd be doing her a favor.

My dad could co-sign too, so perhaps a co-cosigner would be doubly amusing. The less responsibility attached to my name, the better.

I change my disposition as I listen to everything the guidance counselor says. I even comment on the beautiful weather. Now he truly believes that I want to turn my life around and get my grades up, and eventually writes my name down on a piece of paper (even though his eyes are still focused on the computer screen) and promises me he'll contact a few of my teachers and discuss additional measures. Then we can all delight in our delusion, in the myth that's been perpetuated long before our birth.

Sooner or later, they'll see how absurd life is. But until then, I'll play along. I'll tackle college for the same reason people climb Mount Everest: Because it's there.

Mount Everest is in Nepal, in case you didn't learn that in college.

ㅁㅁㅁ

I'm leaving the guidance counselor's office, determined to arrive at English class with a fresh mind and renewed interest. It's never too late, he said, and he was right. It may be too late for him to grow hair, but overall the mantra applies.

So here I am, wandering halls, when Eddie playfully taps me on the shoulder. He's been giving me the creeps ever since I met him, but I turn to face his freckles with a smile. If he were twenty years older and married with children, I'd do him.

"How are you?" he says.

"Fine."

"Good."

And he just walks beside me like that, giving me the most nervous smile I've ever seen. I quickly recall that he has sent me several Facebook messages in the past few days. I've replied to most of them, but not all. My guess is that he wants to talk about the ones I didn't reply to, but he surprises me.

"So now that you're gay, do you want to really hang out?"

"I was always gay, fool."

"But now everyone knows."

"Yeah, so what." I lean in to whisper. "Are you gay too?"

He tilts his head downward a bit, still smiling. God, this kid creeps me out. He's crushing on me way too hard. I ask him why he hasn't come out already, and he cites a lack of strength or courage or something wimpy like that. It's his life, and he won't take control. No way in hell can I relate to someone who doesn't take control of his own life, someone who takes no responsibility for his actions.

"Come on, let's hang out," he says. He actually grabs my upper arm.

"Dude, get off me."

He looks at me, petulant and confused. I want to smack the freckles from his face, but alas, there are too many students here. In an empty hallway, however, I could get away with it. I slapped Misty, so now I'm primed to slap Eddie twice as hard. When you know what someone wants, you can get away with a lot.

"Will you meet me at the gym tonight? Please?"

Eddie's more buff than I, so we'll cross paths in the gym eventually.

"Yes? I guess."

"Terrific."

"Wipe your face. You're drooling," I say, and power forward to English class, disgusted.

□□□

Clint's still sitting next to me in English, where I first met him, because Mr. K assigned seats to everyone based on where we sat on the second week of the school year. The strictures of academia, it seems. Turgid, rigid, glacial ... and no one can quickly adapt to a system with those mechanisms in place, including me. Right now, I need to adapt.

Clint's been talking–flirting–with Misty and I'm not okay with that. He knows that, and I know that she's the reason everyone knows my little secret. It's frustrating that I had to hear it from someone else.

Next to Clint, I'm tiny, but that's changing as I stick to my fitness regimen. Cereal bar after fruit after dead lift after oatmeal package after squat thrust after ... If I were gay and thin, I'd definitely be bullied.

The least he could do is admit that he helped leak my secret, but he doesn't. I had him pegged as someone who wouldn't reveal secrets that might hurt his closest friends, but alas, I must not be a close friend.

No problem.

He serves no purpose now, except for giving his heffer screaming orgasms. And hey, if Misty's new squeeze keeps her away from me, all the better. I guess I am pleased with their arrangement.

Mr. K asks me about the significance of Hamlet's final soliloquy, and I say, "What line?"

Totally caught off guard. What a great start to a better report card. Clint raises his hand and answers. The teacher agrees, praising his articulate response. I'll be damned if Clint the Lummox has a brain. Spending so much time watching from the sidelines must give him plenty of chances to read.

□□□

Lunchtime banter holds my interest for once. The guys are talking about the most recent episode of *Cambrian Lore*. This time, I'm able to contribute. See, I'm progressing in every facet of my education, including social. If you're not one of them, then you'll try to be like them. Thanks to my hard work, I no longer have to try. I am.

After lunch and Study Hall, I will carry my work-hard attitude to the next class.

"If you rewind it halfway, to the part where they're falling down the slope, you can kind of see her giant pussy lips." Zack chugs the rest of his apple juice and belches.

"I'll be sure to check that out, dude," Mike says, visibly astonished by this revelation. I hope a hot chick invites him over and astonishes him with her beauty, and then sexually ravages him, begging to get fucked bare, spreading her herpes. We will then see true astonishment when the itching starts.

"I'll check that out too," Eddie says.

"You're so full of it," I say, trying to make him squirm. Before he turns too red, I say, "Do you even have cable?"

The whole table laughs.

Eddie rubs my leg, but says loudly enough for everyone to hear, "Thanks, Jude. Thanks a lot. Everyone knows I have cable. Geez."

He's still rubbing my leg, and I should shoo him away, but I like the hardness. His hands are so rough, they're blue collar. Young blue collar. Apprentice. They haven't lifted enough bricks, repaired enough toilets, slapped enough girlfriends. They never will, most likely.

Eddie adds a foot to the mix, playing footsie. He's much more daring than I thought.

I stand. "Excuse me, guys. Bathroom."

I have to cool down before Study Hall. The bathroom is a buffer between the expectations of teachers and students. It's where a guy can let his dick hang out and breathe, just for a minute.

Eddie sets his empty tray atop the garbage can. I imagine he'll be joining me.

When one door closes, another opens. Or is it a window? Misty and Clint are pretty much out of the picture right now. Eddie's taking their place. He'll be driven away just like the others, but until then, I'll have my fun.

ㅁㅁㅁ

At home, the costume has arrived. The packaging gets torn away, strewn about the living room floor, and I rip the contents from the boxes.

Mom snatches the keys and takes the Camaro. My social circle has expanded so rapidly, I no longer care if she takes the car.

The horns accentuate my personality. The mesh shirt reveals a faint shadow of my nipples. The cape highlights my dominance. The black Speedo holds me in place. These pieces, when combined, make me look very gay, but at least they hide the bruises from last weekend. If people were unsure of my sexuality before, they'll soon learn. Everyone should be themselves, even on Halloween.

ㅁㅁㅁ

Eddie Fischer insists on driving. He's been persistent, and his perseverance is kind of inspiring. There's a lesson in there somewhere, about never giving up. The fat receptionist punches our membership cards and down the stairs we go. The place reeks of sweat and sanitizer, as always, but this time I see no sign of Misty. Figures. The gym was her last ditch attempt at getting in my pants, and when that failed, she took her fat ass somewhere more likely to inspire awe. Clint's bedroom. I actually cringe when I see the now-empty elliptical machine where she once stood.

Eddie takes the treadmill next to mine and talks over the hum of his machine, even though I have my headphones in. If Bobby would stumble upon us, that'd be a great three-way session. He may not like me, but another young and reasonably cute freckled face like Eddie's might convince the man to double dip, to break the law on multiple accounts, because hey, you only live once. His life's ruined enough by a frumpy wife and that drooling baby of his. To stay young, he must fuck young. Men are wired to fuck young. I don't have to try.

Burning calories has helped my appetite. I decide to treat Eddie nicer for the duration of our workout, because then he might be willing to buy me a protein bar. Eddie prances from one machine to the next, and I warn him about exhaustion, dehydration and muscle failure. It's the thought that counts. Should he become injured, I can at least say that I warned him. Will I provide bedside consolation? No, fuck no.

Eddie scribbles his progress as if he's training for a body-building competition. I admire that precision. It must be the combination of glasses, freckles and red hair. A queer Irish jock-nerd. Then again, I do the exact same thing at home, and I'm nothing like him. I pick his brain to make him feel important.

"What math are you taking?"

"AP," he grunts, "Calculus. You?"

"Math 12, but I'm not doing so well. I might need a tutor."

"Please don't tell me you're trying to be a dumb jock." He sets the barbell down and sits up, leaving splotches of sweat where his neck and shoulders touched base. "Dumb jocks are so last decade."

"I'm getting As in everything else. I just don't understand the numbers. I don't get anything Mrs. D is talking about."

"Do you have a learning disability?" He actually winks when he asks, but I remain silent. He wiggles his nose, sneezes, and then reverts to a dour expression. Trying to play it cool. "I can tutor you, if you want. I'd love to help you out."

"Thanks, Eddie. You know, sometimes I don't realize how lucky I am to have friends like you and Clint and the rest. I really appreciate you all taking me under your wing."

"And what a small wing it's becoming, as you continue to grow. I mean, look at you." He takes his own verbal cue as an excuse to gawk at my body. "You're building up nicely."

"I learn from the best."

"Sure do. One day, you might even be teaching us a thing or two."

"Oh, I hope so. I really do."

Sunday, October 27

I relent at Mom's request to attend church, not because I'm sympathetic to her aim, but because it's respite from Eddie, who's been hounding me all weekend. Calls, texts, direct messages. I can't take it anymore, so I switch up the routine. A diversified life is a happy one, or so I've heard. A bunch of crap, really, because a happy life is one in which you're popular. Jesus Christ was probably happy.

Of course, there's nothing special about our church. Compared to European churches, ours is an atrocity. All white with a grey steeple and a non-functioning bell. Not a stained glass window in sight. It might as well be a house, for all the flavor it adds to the construction dotting Main Street.

None of those bland features discourages the church's adherents, however, because the parking lot is loaded with cars of all models. Mom parks near the dumpster. We head toward the rear entrance. We step over Big Gulps and broken glass.

There should be a whiff of salt in the air, because a church would have to be located near the ocean to have so much rust on its generator and gutters. So many abandoned sandals and old T-shirts, as if we're in the city, as if donation clothes fell out of the garbage bags used to transport them to the donation box. The aesthetic is missing, but the charm is there. On the inside, right?

The inside is no better. Watching the churchgoing masses in their preferred environment is unsettling. Every week they gather, ready to worship something they can't see, something they can't prove, and yet they neglect the church's aesthetic.

It doesn't have to be the Ritz, it just has to be good enough to carry out His will, Hallelujah.

You can immediately tell who's rich and who's poor. The well-to-do sit up front, wearing proper church attire. From the back pew, where I sit, I can see a blond-haired girl holding a customized yellow parasol. Yes, it brings out her sun dress. Yes, she's sitting up front.

I'm wearing a shirt from Goodwill. It's brown and has a hole near the armpit. If I work hard, my muscle growth will widen that hole. I'll Hulk the shirt. The shirt's too small as it is. I have to keep pulling it down to cover my lower back, an area that sees the public more often than I'd like. American Eagle, Ralph Lauren and Lacoste need to be washed. Maybe I could have dressed better. Oh well. God should be happy I even showed up.

The chatter settles down as the pastor flicks the microphone and says the grey weather is a great excuse to be indoors, praising the Lord. He sounds like someone worth paying attention to. Not. Being here should keep Mom off my back for at least a week. There's no rule that says I have to pay attention. Variety really is the spice of life.

Observing the yellow-stained walls and builder-grade columns gives me an air of self-importance, because I know I'm a better person than the people who built this. For all the taxes a church is able to dodge, you'd think they'd update such slipshod interiors. Exteriors.

Bad taste infects every square inch.

Then there's Kristen McNicky.

She's sitting in the second pew, perky as can be. No one else from school, just her, dressed like she was born to praise God Almighty. During praise and worship, she stands and sways her hips, following the tunes emitted from the black speakers, not even reading the projected lyrics. Yes, there's a projector. All that's missing is a disco ball and strobe lights. Clear the pews and turn this place into a roller skating rink. Skate for Jesus.

I mumble the lyrics, standing still so my shirt doesn't rise. Seeing my acceptance of ceremony, my mom cries. Surrounding followers touch her lightly, smiling. This had better get me into heaven.

Blah, blah. That's what the pastor sounds like right before he asks for tithing money. Mom forks over five bucks without question, saying to me, "This is for the Lord."

This is for your college fund, she was supposed to say. This is for you.

At the end of service, people swarm the lobby area for after-service chit-chat. Perhaps the only time when the rich and the poor see eye to eye is when they share a common religion, an ideology, a philosophy.

This baffles me, because when I see these same people at the mall, there are those who carry more than one shopping bag and those who do not. That's the divide. One group does not converse with the other. They shop in different stores and set different budgets; there's no mutual interest. But throw an invisible man and some cooked-up fables into the mix, and the money, no matter whose it is, goes to a greater good. The masses have that in common. They allow themselves to become mind slaves, droning in and out of consciousness at the pastor's command. When he says Amen, they waken from their hypnotized states long enough to repeat it.

I almost feel bad for Kristen McNicky–and that's a big almost–but it's not like she had a choice. As a child, she was likely spoon fed this garbage until she grew up to believe it, and now, without any spiritual maturity, she accepts the teachings of her childhood as indisputable fact. She doesn't consider that, if maybe she'd been born in India, she'd believe in a different god.

Not my problem. Actually, it works in my favor, because now I have a way in. Kristen, who was aloof and inaccessible at school, is now smiling and exuberant here in this carpeted, low-ceilinged lobby.

Thanks but no thanks, Alyssa. I've found my own way to Kristen's heart. I'll hold it in my hands until I win Prom King, and then crush it. Until then, she can live in denial by believing that her existence has meaning. She can question her faith when I'm done with her. I just have to keep the spell going long enough for her to believe that I am good and want to change. She can help me change. That's every woman's fantasy, right? To change a man?

Thursday, October 31

Really hyper today. Watch out, I'm stoked.

Been spending a lot of time with Eddie these past few weeks. He's insatiable. No matter how much of my attention he receives, he wants more. He's almost worse than Misty.

He's been coming over enough to arouse Mom's suspicion. She definitely acknowledges his presence, because he's a good boy who reminds her of a life she might've had, if only she'd had better judgment in choosing a man.

He's slept over, too. We shared the bed, and yeah, there was some touching, but nothing too serious. Not my type at all, so it's best to keep him at a distance. He'll always beg for more; who knows, it might be nice to wake up to the sound of him playing the lute or something equally magical. Not what I'd get from Robert Desmond, that's for sure.

Eddie still likes to keep his emotional distance during lunch. It's up to him to come out of the closet. Can't help him there. Build up the courage or stay away from me. Actually, I don't really care whether he comes out, but constantly reminding him of how repressed he is makes him feel inferior. It's something I have that he doesn't.

The guys do ask about him, though. When he's in the bathroom, they ask if he's applying makeup.

I ask them what they know about Eddie, and they say everything, because they all grew up together. Yeah, that's not the same thing, I say. Eddie doesn't speak much during lunch, and if not during lunch, then when?

Well, maybe he should start. We're not stopping him.

I'll get him to talk, if you want me to.

Why does he talk to you so much?

How should I know? Maybe we have a lot in common. Anyway, he'll come out of his shell.

With all these narcissistic personalities at one table, it's no wonder Eddie crosses his legs in an X, hands in lap, waiting for affirmation. That desperate need to be desired, to be popular–at least we have that in common. He pushes me in the gym, and that's good too. Gym's always better with a partner. Not a life partner, but a partner.

It's official: Eddie spends way too much time with me before, during, in-between and after classes.

Truthfully, I'd like to spend more time with Zack Eldin, because he can teach me swings and passes. Because of the few remaining days of outdoorsy weather, lacrosse ranks high on my priority list. Outdoorsy weather is subjective, though. The Native Americans played in the snow.

To be honest, I'd much rather dress as a Native American than Satan, but my bruises are still visible. Either way, it doesn't cost me anything, so I can't complain.

□□□

Eddie likes my costume, and I'd like his too if he weren't pussying out. He played it safe with a jock outfit–hardly a costume at all. To spruce up the look, he should wear less. A jock strap and a jersey, that's it. Then again, he's a tennis player, so feebleness is to be expected.

Took some beers from the fridge, because Mom's not watching. Added two changes of clothes to the Camaro's trunk, because Mom's not watching. She'll bring it to me later. Check, check. Ready to go.

Now we're standing by the door, Eddie and me, waiting for Alyssa Zaianassey to pick us up. Eddie's wearing contacts, so that his helmet fits.

Porch lights are off to discourage trick-or-treaters, who would be appalled by Mom in her natural state–witch. She should lie on the couch playing Candy Crush rather than hand out candy. That would be to everyone's advantage. One more Halloween spent watching horror movies. One more Halloween closer to her miserable death.

Keeping the porch lights off also disguises the ugliness of our house, which is actually a rental. Given the budget and fixed income, we're lucky to be renting. Eddie grabs my butt and I let him. Alyssa's driver pulls into the driveway. I dash outside so she doesn't get a good look at my shack.

Eddie has no choice but to quickly follow, because otherwise I'll kill him, maybe, and say it was the ghost of Halloween. We hop in the car with our candy bags (filled with beers) and Alyssa sternly says to the driver, as if we're in an action movie: "Drive." We're gone in ten seconds flat, no lie. Time to roll, to rock, to run, to outmaneuver the establishment, Sheriff Roswell, cavity creeps, monstrous children, protected sex ...

Beguiled by the bile I'm going to produce, I quiver when my bare legs and semi-bare back press against the leather seat. Threads entwined around Eddie Fischer's frame ensconce him in safety, and the pampered princess in the passenger seat has heating vents blowing at her face. Her straight black hair doesn't move.

"You're dressed as a maid?" I say.

"Do I look like a Filipina? *Puk gai*! No, no. I am a French maid. There is a big difference." Her accent slips out after having spoken in tongues.

"Oh no, of course. You're right."

Meanwhile, Eddie sits quietly, hands in lap, like a behaved child. More than likely feels ashamed of his crotch, which he bared on camera and sent to me in a moment of weakness. His weakness empowers me, his horniness compels me. How could it not? Free and easy opportunities abound in this capitalist country.

"Eddie, say something nice."

"Like what?"

"Say something about her hair."

Alyssa flips it like Farrah Fawcett, fluttering her tiny lashes.

"Your hair is very pretty," Eddie says.

The driver coughs and for the first time takes one gloved hand from the wheel long enough to curl his mustache.

"Thank you, Eddie. I like your costume too, even if it does remind me of Connor's jersey costume. I can't believe he's still with her."

"Who?" It's fun to play dumb.

"Kristen, duh. They're like, still together, for like, two and a half years. Can you believe that? Two and a half years?"

"I bet they don't even go to the same church."

"I hate gossip," Eddie says.

"Shut up, Eddie," Alyssa says. "Just kidding, but I really do like your costume. I thought you play tennis?"

He nods but she's already looking at me again before she can examine him.

"And you really are a devil!"

"Do I look like a devil to you? Jesus Christ. I *am* the devil. I am Satan." The driver cackles, seemingly unconcerned that his laugh is too loud for this car, too out of place. Eddie and Alyssa force nervous smiles.

Outside, it is pitch dark even as we pass a densely populated neighborhood. Perhaps serial killers are on the loose, cutting power supplies and taking the lives of the want-to-bes. Sadly, I am one of those want-to-bes, but no one has to know that. I will graduate to serial killer one day. They live on a higher plane of consciousness, otherwise, why would they do it? At the very least, it has to be fun. When adult life becomes weighed down by jobs, dinner parties, weddings and funerals, homicide seems like the only escape, the only way to feel alive again. It's what it means to be a human being.

All I can do is strive to become better at what I do. At the party, I will be the devil, the one and only Satan. In acting thus far, I've demonstrated competence.

Deceiving everyone, each and every day, means that I am adept.

❏❏❏

The party's packed when we arrive, because we're cool

enough to show up late. Kristen might be another hour. Connor's already here. Our spot in the chain, the hierarchy, is gold but not platinum. Now's the time to waver from one inebriated island to the next, taking sips at each.

The costumes are diverse, and although several of my classmates are dressed as characters from *Cambrian Lore*, none of them is dressed the same. I know that because I've seen all four seasons now. Because I am prepared to win.

Alyssa disappeared the moment she walked through the door, predictably. She had to make her rounds.

Clint and Misty are snuggled on the living room couch, predictably, and under a comforter because her outfit shows too much skin.

Of course, dressed like a dog, she has every right to be on the sofa. That bitch. She might be getting screwed under the comforter. Who buys electric comforters, anyway? Old people? Misty and Clint have settled in much like old people do, because they finish each other's sentences. I can hear this within earshot. In trying to enervate me, she always comes up short.

Eddie and I avoid hard liquor. I know my limits. I've been trained well; downed a few too many in trying to keep up with Mom, the real competition. Another boring Saturday night, was it not? And yet my dad loses custody. In all unfairness, that's how the world works–under Satan's rule. Right now, this is my party. Man of honor and host Zack Eldin is nowhere to be seen. I'm almost certain he's screwing someone upstairs. He feeds off the social current and follows the stream to the white water where the rafters ride him, pound him with their paddles and give him a concussion that leads to euphoria. If there's a hard drug in the household, he's on it. It's so like him to advance, advance, and not retreat like a spectator whose safety is at the mercy of foul balls. He could back up a bit and cover old ground, much like a tennis player does. He could learn something from Eddie.

Yeah, Eddie's staying in one place. So much time spent with me as to inoculate him from peer pressure. And he started off higher in hierarchy than I, just a couple months ago. Funny how you can surpass someone and leave them begging for the secret, but by the time they find out, time will have passed too quickly and they will be lost. I will allow him to be lost.

I ditch him, tell him to drink more beer. Fuck it, you're not wearing glasses tonight, might as well get a little tipsy. Else why'd you come here in the first place? Let go of my leg. Let go.

Kristen McNicky can be seen at the front entrance, among the mess of leaves and shoes. Ho boy, what a mess to clean up in time for Zack's parents, but then again, his mommy is a pushover. I push over a vase and watch the shards skate across the laminate wood flooring, because oops, I can.

I don't even know how it happens, despite being stone cold sober, but I've somehow found myself in a game of dice with Elmer Fudd, Frankenstein's monster, Tinkerbell in drag and a 1920's detective with a bubble pipe. The detective has put the bubble pipe down as his bet, and the rest have only vowed to drink. I respect the detective for some reason; must be the gall.

I don't put anything down, but notice that the dice have accumulated dust. I wonder how the dice must feel, usually so comfortable in people's hands, but having to pick up dust from the ground, take it with them. Or are human hands worse? So oily and autonomous. The dice never get washed, so they just tumble from one environment to the next, carrying with them the remains of the past. Frankenstein's monster spills PBR everywhere and I stand up to leave, disgusted.

Alyssa the not-Filipina maid is flirting with some jock in the kitchen, no doubt trying to nab him, even though she doesn't have to try. I interrupt. "Everyone here is drunk. It's crazy!"

She smiles at me seductively and pushes the jock aside.

"So what? No one's parents care, least of all Zack's." She takes a shot, as if proving her point required action. Ooh, she's such a badass for drinking alcohol.

"They all have rides."

"I find that hard to believe."

"Everyone here has a DD, dude," the jock says. "Stop being

a wet blanket."

"Okay," I say, glancing back toward the living room where Clint and Misty are canoodling. "I won't be a wet blanket. Happy Halloween!"

Pushing and shoving.

Back to the living room, where Misty's sitting on Clint's lap. Still. She's wearing dog ears on a headband, and a dog's snout over her own, held to her head with an elastic band. Clint's just the opposite. He's wearing cat ears and painted whiskers. They probably thought it was a cute idea to dress up as opposites, when they know it's supposed to be the other way around. For being so delusional, they deserve whatever comes their way, whether it helps or hinders their plunge into the throes of love. No, they don't understand what love is. Much too young.

Eddie's still talking but not drinking. Good. I'd like to keep him that way.

"Hey, Clint," I say. He says hey back.

"How are things, Jude?" Misty says.

"Hey, Clint. At the end of Hamlet, does he actually get poisoned?"

"Kind of, but not the way he was supposed to. Hamlet gets stabbed by a poisoned dagger, courtesy of Laertes, and Gertrude drinks the poisoned drink intended for *Hamlet*."

"Is that why you're not going to drink anything tonight? Come on. Relax, it's Halloween."

"No way, buddy. I'm the designated driver. Connor and Justin and Lee are coming with. Why, are you trying to get me drunk?"

"Don't try to get Clint drunk," Misty says. I glare at her right in front of him. She shuts up.

"I was just wondering what a big guy like you's threshold is, that's all. I bet you wouldn't even get drunk after six beers. Still be able to drive." "Yeah, I bet you're right."

There's an awkward silence that's only awkward because the piece of shit won't drink anything, so I switch up my plans.

"Zack told me to tell you that he found his smash piece,

whatever that means." I know that Clint knows what a smash piece is, because he tries so hard to be worldly and cultural and Canadian; anti-American, really.

"A smash piece, huh?"

"Yeah. He said he told you about it once? That you were supposed to see when it happened?"

"He did, did he?"

This lardass thinks he's so clever with the questions. "Yes. He did."

"Well then, where is he?"

"He's upstairs in his bedroom, but he wants you to go see before it's over."

"Baby," Misty says. "Don't go. Stay here with me until they're ready."

"And how will I know that they're ready if I'm sitting here and he's upstairs? Let me go check. I'll be right back."

"Baby, wait."

Clint stands up from the couch after he gently pushes Misty off. The whole cratered mess doesn't return to buoyancy right away, and I almost want to laugh; the stupid fat cow (dog, whatever) sits there with her tail between her legs. With no one to cling to, she has no grounding, and so she heads straight to the bathroom. To cry, I hope.

"Eddie, get ready to leave soon," I say. He gives a sheepish nod, because the party would be boring without me by his side.

Clint's upstairs, where I know he'll be pressured to drink. His inhibitions can be set loose easily, but his morality is seldom shaken. He's the giant pillar about to fall and crack the cement.

I head upstairs, and he's already drinking. Everything's a lot easier without women, including getting drunk. No Misty to hold him back or say it's not a good idea. Life's so much easier.

They're looking through Zack's drawers for childhood photos, and Zack doesn't much mind, because they're all laughing like idiots. I casually step into the bedroom and Clint says, "Oh, Jude. Look what have you done to me."

I almost feel embarrassed for him.

"Well, it's a party. Have fun."

"But they need a ride home." He points to a wall, by which I mean he's pointing in Connor's general direction.

"I'll find someone. If worst comes to worst, we can get Alyssa's driver or I can call my mom. No big deal. It's Halloween." I'm quite proud of myself. "Relax."

"Good point."

"Yeah," Zack chimes in. "Relax."

◻◻◻

All it takes is twenty minutes for the cats of inhibition, morality and judgment to go straight out the window and onto the street, where they will be run over by a driver who doesn't much care about hitting the brakes. Or paying attention.

Out of the twenty-six people at this party, nineteen of them are plastered and ready to pass out. Two have vomited. Half of them are first-timers. All great fun, but I've invoked the competitive spirit of the football team so greatly that they're playing truth or dare and choosing dare every time.

One of them has streaked, one has urinated into a vase, and one is currently eating a whole bowl of chips, which seems the wimpiest of the three, but what do I care.

"Remember health class when we had to use beer goggles?" I say. The six of them nod, but I only care that Connor is one of the six, so that the rest will follow his lead. He is. "Is this better or worse than the beer goggles?"

"Way better," Connor says.

"Definitely better," Batman says.

"Yeah, definitely," Sherlock Holmes says.

"I bet you can't parallel park," I say.

Connor touches his chin and looks up, though his eyes wander from light bulb to ceiling plaster to corner to lamp to … like he's actually considering the challenge. It's almost too easy. He's really going to do it.

"Dare," Connor says.

"I didn't even dare you!"

"I can do it."

"Dude," Sherlock says. "No way."

"I can do it. Come on, watch me do it."

I brandish Clint's car keys, because why the hell not. He's already toppled over and it's just a quick swipe. No reason not to. I hand them to Connor, telling him to use Clint's van. Connor Welbach can do as he pleases because Clint's already said it was fine, or else what are bros good for, right?

If I'm lucky, they'll wreck the car. It's not really a party until something gets wrecked, and the vase I shattered doesn't cut it. Sometimes havoc doesn't need a reason. It's just fun.

Yes, they're really going to do it. All I have to do is sit at the bay window and watch before calling it in.

"Wait," I say. "Before you go, you'll need some liquid courage. Everybody." Vodka shots for everyone else, nothing for me. My red cup's empty. They imbibe and I sneer behind my raised cup. They're going down. "All right, now we're all ready."

They're too stoked to hear me at this point. All I have to do is show them the front door, but Connor takes the lead.

Once they're outside, I immediately head to the land line mounted on the kitchen wall. Bad enough that it has a cord, so I have to be quick. I phone home. Mom doesn't pick up til the last ring because I've woken her, I can tell, and her voice sounds hoarse, as if she's been screaming at a corn plow to stop before it runs her over.

"Mom, I need you to pick me up. I don't feel comfortable here. Some people are doing drugs and I just want to come home."

"Baby, where are you? Where are you? Hello?"

"At Zack's Halloween party." I give her the address and explain the location in relation to landmarks, because she's too stupid to read a map or listen to her phone's GPS, and it's too late for her to ask directions. I have to be saved right this second. "Please, can you hurry over? Eddie's here with me too."

"I'm coming right now. Are you or Eddie hurt? Should I

call the police?"

"No, we're fine. No one's hurt. Just come pick me up. I hate it here."

"I'm on my way. Sit tight."

Now I only have to wait and hope (for once) that she's not too fucked up to operate a motor vehicle, because she's had strikes against her before. She'll make it now, though, because her only child's life is at stake, and for some reason that's only of priority when death is imminent, but never during the lulls of life, those quiet moments at breakfast when she lights her cigarette using the gas stove. Or when she forgets to lock the door before bed, but brushes it off the next morning with some excuse like, "We have nothing worth stealing anyway."

Now it's too late for her to win Mother of the Year, but she'll come around. She might even win bonus points if she arrives within the next ten minutes. I think she'll make it. Even an idiot can take three main roads and two side streets without getting lost. It's not that hard.

I alternate between watching the clock and watching the boys outside. They're all in Clint's van, and Connor's driving. The rest of them are just monkeys who think they're more sober than he.

Clint's still passed out.

At minute eight, I head to the kitchen and dial 9-1-1, citing a drunk driving incident. I use a sloppy, imitated voice (Clint's) and report a stolen vehicle.

"The driver is drunk, I think. He was swerving."

"Do you know the license plate? Make and model?"

With my cell phone's pictures open, I flip to the cluster of license plate photos that I took and find the one with the rustiest exterior, definitely Clint's. I already memorized the numbers, but it doesn't hurt to double check. I make the operator's job easier by blurting the make and model.

"Great. And where did you last see your vehicle?"

She gets the address, but I mention a different house number. One close by. She'll know that it's a party, at least, because the music's playing in the background. She'll also know that

I've had a few drinks, but in no way have I even considered driving tonight. No, they just stole my car and that's it. "Help is on the way. Please remain calm and stay where you are."

Click.

I grab Eddie by the jersey and pull him out the door just as Mom pulls up in the Camaro. We dash for it and I yell to her through the window to pop the trunk first.

She hesitates, then fumbles for the lever. I seat Eddie inside and grab the clothes from the trunk so that we can change, just in case.

We wait until the cluster of tract homes are two turns and two roads away before changing into our new clothes. Mom looks at me, possibly wondering why I might want to wear a mesh shirt that reveals so much, even on Halloween, and Eddie simply does as he's told. I leave the mesh shirt on and pull over a white T-shirt, followed by a black jacket.

Eddie, from his spot in the back seat, maneuvers into the trunk and puts his football jersey and shoulder pads and helmet and other equipment in there. He does this only after changing into the shirt and raincoat I've provided for him.

"You haven't been drinking, have you?"

"No, Mom."

"What about you?"

"No, ma'am."

"Don't call me ma'am."

"Okay."

"You boys sure you're all right?"

"Yes," I say, growing irritated. "We're just tired."

"Glad to hear that."

She speaks levelly and doesn't swerve, which is a shocking relief to me because when we hit the last stop light, Sheriff Roswell pulls up beside us, looks straight at us, and I don't know what Eddie's doing, but I keep looking forward, straight ahead. I knew Roswell would be on the prowl. Halloween must be a busy time for police.

I love myself for having foresight.

The light turns green and Mom presses the gas, jolting the

car forward.

"Mom! You see the cop right there."

"What is he gonna do? Arrest me for pressing the gas on green?"

"You want to take the chance?"

"Guys," Eddie interjects, "he's not following us. We're in the clear."

"Good," I say.

"I bet they're really on the prowl tonight," Mom says.

"Sure are," Eddie says.

We arrive home way after curfew, undetected. If Sheriff Roswell saw us, he didn't seem to care. The night calls for chaos elsewhere, so why waste time pestering a boy who is not in costume, being driven by his mother?

Eddie's phone chimes.

"Guys," Eddie says, "The party we were just at got busted. Big time."

I check my phone to confirm his statement.

"Well, I'm just glad you boys know better. I've raised a good kid. And Eddie, you're—"

"Oh my God." Eddie's voice cracks. "Connor. The van he was driving."

"What?" I say.

"He crashed it into a tree."

Suddenly, a wailing ambulance, fire truck and police car can be heard.

"Oh, that's awful," I say. "I hope they're okay."

A text from Alyssa Zaianassey comes through: "I know what you did. ;)"

Wink.

Friday, November 1

Mrs. D is supposed to give us a quiz on logarithmic functions, but now she's telling us that we have to postpone it, thanks to yet another special announcement from Principal Snow.

Seniors head to the gym first, followed by the juniors and so on.

I approach Clint, because everything has to appear normal. He can't suspect me of anything, and if I let the guys have too much alone time without me, they'll talk about me. I used to say that, no matter what, women find a way to talk to each other, but sadly I must assume that of my own sex as well.

Clint's not saying much, and I'm guessing he's only nervous about any accusations that might fly. Or if he'll be made an example of. The outcome doesn't matter as long as I am vigilant and have verisimilitude on my side. Clint doesn't. He's crumbling and Misty's not around to squeeze his gut and call him a Teddy Bear. I've stolen his innocence, shaken his confidence.

Mike joins Clint, Eddie and me, but Zack's nowhere to be found. I look across the room for signs of Connor Welbach and Kristen McNicky. I look in the same spot they were sitting last time. They aren't here today.

Principal Snow ruffles some papers and lectures us on the dangers of drunk driving, texting and driving–basically, he speaks out against having fun, burying the lead for as long as possible, and then he finally says it: Connor Welbach was sent to the hospital after suffering injuries to the leg and forehead.

Apparently the visor was pulled down when he wrecked the

car. Connor should have been scalped.

The other guys in the back seat came out either unscathed or with minor injuries, but I can tell that Clint's feeling the pressure. It was his van, after all. Safety first, right? Legal issues and insurance don't matter a lick, not yet. At least no one else got hurt. Now can we please just go home to our worried parents, who will rob us of all privileges in the name of safety?

Clint's looking down, seemingly ashamed of himself. If that's true, then he can't confront me. After all, it was his choice to drink. An objective viewer might blame his decision on peer pressure, but there aren't any legal repercussions for peer pressure. Action triumphs.

Check.

Now I need to keep Eddie at bay, maybe practice math on my own. I understand most of the concepts, but still haven't taken the ACT.

Getting into the right college doesn't matter so much as getting into a college. Top ten schools were never a possibility to begin with, so there's no bottom. I could even complete a few semesters of community college and transfer. Anyone can do that. No wasted afternoons with pencils to paper, being timed, being allowed to drink nothing more than water from a clear bottle, no bathroom breaks permitted once the timer has started.

The most disappointing part of this mandatory meeting in the auditorium is that there's no sign of our school mascot, the Royal Ocelot. No school spirit to speak of. Last night's tragedy really hit home. Boo hoo.

When we're dismissed, the four of us split up and head to our respective classes, but I don't step past the gym exit before Alyssa grabs me by the shirt and says, "Hey, you! We need to talk."

There's no escaping this talk. It's a loose end that worries me.

◻◻◻

Alyssa must have ears everywhere. She tells me exactly what my plan was, and that I set Connor up. That's all well and good, but she hates Kristen and Connor as much as I do, so she agrees to keep it under wraps. I don't do anything more than nod, for semantical reasons; I can later say, "I never said that." My love-hate relationship with Kristen stems from my jealousy, I admit. For the longest time she was the most popular girl in school, and apparently she still is. On that same note, being in her social circle will elevate my own status, so I can't dismiss her outright. Alyssa hates her because she's a girl. Girls are always fighting over something. Oh well. If I can use Alyssa's hatred of Kristen to get ahead, then great.

The rest of the day goes by without a bang. I guess the cops really believe that Clint made the 9-1-1 call. Clint has already admitted to it, either out of guilt or embarrassment. He's quite the stoic.

Eddie, on the other hand, is growing restless and anxious, and is starting to ask questions when he's not being spoken to, just out of the blue. I'll drip feed him the content, but I won't like it. I have a C in math now, so it's not like I need him.

□□□

Now, after school, Eddie twiddles his thumbs while sitting on my bed, like a patient waiting for a prostate exam. Literally twiddling his thumbs. I scoot toward him.

"You have nothing on your walls," he says.

"A blank slate keeps my mind open to new things."

"New things like what?"

"Anything you want."

"What is that even supposed to mean? You never listen to what I want."

"Look, I just don't like clutter. Is that a crime?"

"No, but I get the feeling you've committed a few crimes recently. Should I even ask?"

"I don't know. Should you? Are we married or something?"

"No, we're not," he says. "Thankfully."

"I thought you liked me." I turn away from him and look down, giving my best impression of a disappointed child.

"Sometimes I wonder about you."

"Me? There's nothing to wonder about. I'm out of the closet and now I'm completely out in the open, exploring my personality. For the first time in my life, I feel free to do anything. Ed, I grew up in a shitty house–and look, I'm still here–under the tyranny of abusive parents. My mom never notices me unless I'm bruised, and she's only just recently gotten better because we've been going to church." The tears come slowly; I've had to refrain from blinking for seventy seconds to achieve this effect. "Ed, I'm just ... I'm sorry if you don't like me. I'm trying really hard to figure this all out, but it's hard. When you come out of the closet, you'll see."

He sits there, staring straight ahead. The words have hit him hard, because he's conscious of his swallowing. Couldn't tell you how I know, but I just do. He's aware of his swallowing, and his awareness makes me more aware of my own awareness. He's going to grovel at any moment.

"Jude, I'm so, so sorry. It's just the stress of the party last night. I don't know. I'm sorry."

"Well, shit, you really scare me sometimes. It's like you're not even on my side."

He's shaking now, and his skin has reddened so as to clash with his freckles and orange hair. For once, his glasses are a positive distraction. The green and white striped shirt neutralizes the effect, but it's better than no shirt.

"So," I continue. "Whose side are you on? I've been keeping your secret for a while now. The ball's in your court. I'm here, vulnerable, spilling my feelings, and all you're doing is sitting there on my bed, the very bed I invited you to, practically ignoring me. Being insensitive. I thought we–"

"What?" he yells. "You thought what? You thought I loved you?"

The words hang in the air, and for a second I wonder if Mom overheard anything. We are both too stunned to move an inch, but we maintain eye contact nonetheless. The setting sun sheds a light on his cheeks, eliminating blotchy freckles, making him more angelic. Not that he's my type, but I give credit where it's due. Of course, I can't say that out loud, or he'll pester me for more approval.

We all want things we can't have. I, for one, still don't have his body, and I wonder if that's the reason he likes me; my frame is more slender than his, but I'm taller. Maybe if I hit the gym harder, his feelings will wane. It's worth a shot.

"You what?" I playfully bump my dangling left foot against his right.

"You heard me."

"Well, that certainly changes things, now doesn't it."

"I guess it does."

There's another awkward silence, because he's expecting a reflective response. He won't get one of those, but I fill the gap with something else. "I don't know how I feel right now. There's a lot going on. I have to think."

"Don't say anything if you don't mean it." He bumps my foot with his.

"Oh, I only speak my mind with the best of intentions. That's why we're having this heart-to-heart." I stand up and stretch my arms out, revealing my navel.

"Well, this certainly changes things. I like it." The words are forced, so hard to spit out, but I trudge on because Prom Kings face lots of adversity. Actually, they don't. The votes end up being nigh unanimous.

"Got any dinner? I'm starving," Eddie says, trying to change the subject.

That's the smartest thing he's said all day. Four hours have gone by without food. I need to up my caloric intake, fast.

"First answer me this: What do you know about last night? Be honest."

"You want an honest answer?"

"I just said that."

"Well, these are just rumors. Not wide-spread, but–"

"Who spread these rumors?"

"Alyssa Z."

That bitch. "And she told you to tell me that she knows something about me? How cryptic. I'm going to talk to her."

"Yes, you should." Eddie matter-of-factly states, "She didn't have anything nice to say."

I shrug my shoulders and nonchalantly gesture toward the open door, where I see Mom's eye through the crack.

□□□

Mom's insisted on talking to me and Eddie, because although she's very open-minded, she doesn't like the thought of AIDS. In my entire life, the thought of contracting a venereal disease has not occurred to me, but she swears that it will happen. Eddie looks even more uncomfortable than I am, and I almost wish Sheriff Roswell busted us last night at that intersection. At least we'd be having a serious discussion now.

I grab a Pop Tart and start munching. I have to gain a few more pounds and then stop. I've developed my exercise and nutrition habits to match a regimen you might find in Men's Fitness magazine.

"Eddie, I'm glad you're the one for my Jude. You're perfect for him."

"Mom, stop it. No one even asked you."

"I just can't stand it. You two are so cute."

"Mom, we're not even boyfriends. See what happens when you eavesdrop on conversations? You start hearing things. Then people assume you're crazy." Her smile turns into a flat line. Eddie walks to the refrigerator and opens it, letting some light into the kitchen.

"I just want you to be happy."

"Really? You don't care what I do, just so long as I'm happy?"

Eddie finds a carton of Minute Maid apple juice and punctures the silver circle with the bendable straw.

"No, of course not. Don't be like that."

"Just saying," I say, actually upset that Eddie didn't grab a juice box for me too. "We go to church now, so you don't have to worry too much."

"That doesn't sound quite right, but I'll take it," Mom says.

Once Eddie is sucking air, I decide that that's a natural stopping point for the discussion and grab his hand, luring him far away from my mom. If prodded, she could be an even bigger leak than Alyssa or Misty.

"One more thing," she says, elbows on the table. "Your father just got out of jail. The restraining order has been amended, so he really can't come near us this time. If he does, then he'll be in prison. That's what I really wanted to tell you."

Sure, that's what she really wanted to tell me. Leave it to a woman to make her point (assuming she has one) at the last minute. "Thanks, Mom. I'll keep that in mind." I turn away. "Hey there, boyfriend. Want to hit the gym?"

Eddie pants like a dog, filled with wonder at the sound of Master's command. Like we're going to go for a walk, outside, where both danger and opportunity hide behind smiling facades, the most convincing of which is mine. And, like a dog, he submits.

"Sounds great, Jude."

ㅁㅁㅁ

The receptionist punches my card for the last time before I have to renew. Luckily, I don't need Misty anymore. Eddie's more than willing to pay the price to be my boyfriend. He should only be so lucky. His life would be so ordinary without someone like me reminding him of who he really is. I am his escape.

We run the treadmills and hold a conversation for ten minutes before we run out of breath. Once our muscles are loosened, we do a few stretches on the yoga mats, being very careful not to touch limbs and fall into the temptation of helping each other stretch. I know, it's hard to stay away from someone after you've announced being in a relationship. I believe in delayed gratification.

The crowded gym forces us to work out using the "lats" machines. Under the fluorescent lighting and low ceilings in the town's community weight room, I feel stifled and convince Eddie to bail early.

Before we can make it back up the stairs, however, we encounter Hot Dad. Good old Robert Desmond. He nearly runs right into us, and at this point he has to say something. I won't let him walk around. He'll have to push me in front of all these people.

"Hello, Mr. D. Do you like it when I call you Mister?"

Bobby looks at me with contempt, as if I'm the one who's responsible for making his straight life difficult. As if I'm the one who forced him to marry a frumpy math teacher and breed her until she squirted out a walking reminder of what a horrible fraud he is. At least I'm honest about who I am.

He then looks at Eddie, whom he seems to admire, judging by the way his eyes trail down the exposed U of Eddie's tank top, where a patch of freckles awaits compliment, not touch. Bobby's lips curl into a smile. How primal a smile is! It's deceptively simple and can convey emotions that have nothing to do with happiness. Bobby might as well be one of the cavemen from *Cambrian Lore*.

"Who's your friend?"

Eddie should introduce himself, but he doesn't. Instead of taking initiative, he stands silently beside me with his hands folded in front of him.

"This is Eddie. Why? Do you like what you see?"

"I most certainly do."

Still, Eddie doesn't say anything.

"Well, would you be interested in playing with Eddie?"

He turns to look at me, but still doesn't make a sound. As if his reproachful gasp is supposed to stop me.

"I would be very interested in that."

"How about a threesome then? You can't have him without me."

"Wait a minute," Eddie interjects. I shush him.

"Just for one night, nothing else?"

"Yeah, one night. And then I promise I'll stay away from you, hot as you are. C'mon, just agree to it and let's get this thing done." I grab the bottom of Eddie's tank top and lift it up, revealing toned-but-not-muscular abs. A flat stomach without any visible layer of fat. Shredded. "He acts innocent, but you see that little red garden trail? It leads to a special treasure! He's horny beyond belief. Aren't you?"

"Right now, yeah, but not as much as I used to be. I used to be your age."

"And how old are you, exactly?" Eddie says in a neutral tone, defeated. If he was uncomfortable at all, he would have walked away by now. Exposing his abs to a stranger certainly dehumanized him a bit. I learned that from watching porn; the sooner the director can convince the model to undress, the more the model is likely to perform. Shirt's already off, why not the pants? Might as well remove those socks and undies while you're at it, because the camera's been on for five minutes already.

"Thirty-seven. I'm brutally honest. You get what you see."

"No diseases or drugs?" Eddie's really coming out of his shell.

We have to step aside for two people to walk through the doorway, and then we move the conversation closer to the bathrooms.

"No STDs. The only drug I do is caffeine."

I let them talk. Eddie's the type who will talk once you crack him open. His paranoia will guide him through myriad questions of varying intrusions, the least of which is physical standing. No, he runs the gamut—has to inquire about his marital status, and, gasp, he's married to Mrs. D? The one who teaches math at our school?

"That's enough," I say. "We're all good to go, so let's get on with it."

"Great," Bobby says. "Send me a message."

"I will," I say, waving him off.

Next, I focus my attention on Eddie, who's a little shaken and is scratching his bare arms in worry. I'll have to convince him further, but after having had such a tenuous discussion with a hot scum bag, I can persuade Eddie to do as I please.

If I'm lucky, he'll develop feelings for Bobby instead.

Truthfully speaking, I cannot be around Eddie much longer. He's cramping my style, detracting from my social standing with his meek presence. If he'd just lose the glasses, he'd be so much hotter. He could even win Prom King this year if he plays his cards right, especially now that Connor's been disfigured by stitches. (He'll also be on crutches upon release from the hospital. No more football.)

"If you really do love me, you'll do me this favor."

"Geez, now I don't really know. I'm not good enough?"

"It's not that, but we have our whole lives ahead of us to be monogamous, you know?"

Eddie's face lights up.

"So do me this one favor and then we can be monogamous."

"Deal," he says. He offers a handshake, but I'm already sipping from the water fountain. Boyfriends don't need to shake hands.

Thursday, November 21

The golden Buddha's eyes are squinted. I wonder if there are any Buddha statues with non-squinty eyes. Their eyes are always closed. Or are they just Chinese eyes? This particular Buddha statue fits well on the vanity, where I'm sitting. Although the Buddha is dusty, the makeup and nail polish containers are well organized and glossy. I look at my reflection in the mirror and see Alyssa linger over my left shoulder. She puts one pale hand on my shoulder, and taps with salmon-colored nails.

"It's true. I know what you did," she says.

"Good for you."

"But I'm rooting for you, okay? It's so hard not to. We both want the same thing."

"Which is?"

"Popularity. Or, in your case, notoriety. Wait, that's the word for notorious, right?"

"Yes, that's the noun form."

"Phew," she exhales. "Hey, don't laugh. I'm not as stupid as you think I am."

"How do you know what I think?"

"I can tell. How else would I know what you're up to?"

"Good point," I say.

"You're so obvious," she says.

If she wants popularity, she can have it, and we can discuss those plans right after I leave this chintzy chair and start pacing. I don't like looking at myself in the mirror with her next to me, I've discovered. She makes me look like shit, by anyone's standards. Even Eddie'd have to agree.

"Where do you want to go from here?"

"Wherever," she says. "What did you have in mind?"

"Well, my goal is to win Prom King this year."

Alyssa laughs so hard that she leans against the bedpost for balance. When her face reddens and her eyes grow puffy, I know she's laughed too long, and I want nothing more than to strangle her with her own wiry black hair.

"What?" she screeches. She sounds like a Chinese witch.

"Don't laugh. I'm a lot smarter than you think. I already told you what my goal is, so let's hear yours."

"I just want to get back at Kristen, that's all. She's the school's pageant girl, the precious beauty queen that can do no wrong. The one all the other girls follow. She probably prays right before bed every night. I bet she prays."

"She prays."

"I knew it! Well, that doesn't give her any right to talk down to me like I'm trash. I have feelings too."

"Well, what did you have in mind? You're a lot closer to her than I am."

"That's the thing. She doesn't talk to me that much. She always has these airs about her. Anyway, what do you know so far?" Alyssa's short shorts ride up too far when she sits on the bed, and I can tell that she isn't wearing any undergarments.

"Not much. Just that she goes to church. We go to the same church."

"No *wai*." Her Cantonese accent slipped.

"Way."

"Can I make a suggestion?"

"I'm listening." I stop pacing and perk up.

"Outside of school, when she's not hanging with me or Shannon or anybody like that, she's with the God Squad. What if we could pull her away from that? Know what I mean? Shake her faith a little?"

"I know what you mean."

"Because without her dumb religion, she's nothing. She can't act holier-than-thou anymore. Right?"

I wonder if Buddha is part of a dumb religion. "Right."

Friday, November 22

It's the next morning and I'm staring at yet another (pop) quiz on logarithmic functions, and because I haven't been practicing, I'm rusty. If logs aren't tricks, then I don't know what a trick is. I do the work for all the problems but I doubt I'll pass.

During lunch, I sit with Eddie in the hallway, away from Mike, Zack and Clint, and skirt around the topic of Bobby for as long as I can before he flat out asks me. I go into detail, saying that Bobby shares a past with me, that it was a hot and dirty fling that once Eddie experiences for himself, he will truly appreciate.

He sounds skeptical now, but says he'll go along. For someone who is a gay virgin, he's surprisingly open-minded. Most people want their first time to be special. Well, that's for people with dignity. Whatever dignity he had before, I've taken it away and replaced it with the desire to try something different, to act out, to live an extraordinary, transgressive life. And he's met me halfway, all thanks to the power of love.

□□□

Libraries are strange places. They are supposedly for people who want to read and borrow books, but that's hard to believe when the city library has so many shady characters passing through its doors and staying too long. A building of heat and shelter, free and open to the public, supported by our taxes. A great place to leave your mark all over the bathroom stalls. I am not the worst person here, not even close.

I had to borrow the Camaro, though. I parked three blocks away, just in case someone's tracking me. The man I'm meeting at the library shouldn't have the chance to record my license plate, or make and model. I'm meeting Alyssa's dealer, so I need to be prepared.

Sunday, November 24

Zack shares messages on Facebook about how much it sucks to be grounded, and I consider that to be accurate. Then he posts a photo of Kristen and Connor and himself, as a joke, obviously too stupid to realize that everything he's posted online can be seen by the world, no matter how much he manages his privacy settings. In the photo they are holding red cups.

I'm at a cafe with Eddie as I read these updates. He's bought a strawberry smoothie for me. He asked why I wanted a smoothie on such a cold, gloomy and wet day, and I said a smoothie is the perfect drink for a day like today. One slurp will lift your spirits, or else it will freeze your brain and force you to laugh at how silly a choice it was.

Additionally, it's nice to be different and refrain from ordering hot cocoa like everyone else. I think Eddie really liked that. He likes that I always have something interesting to say. I like that about me too. It's easier to make people agree with you when you surprise them with unexpected responses, rationalities and justifications. They never remember scripted responses that fail to provoke curiosity. Too easy to fall into that trap. One day you're working a job where you have to smile at everyone. "Hello! How are you? Great weather we're having, huh?" The next day you're out of a job and you forget how to surprise people. I won't let that happen to me. If Eddie's smart, he'll heed my warnings and become an outstanding person too. Give them something to talk about and they'll remember you. They might even name you the new Prom King.

He won't retain the lessons I'm gracing him with. He understands that you have to be attractive before they'll listen to you, but he doesn't know what to say. Any monkey can drag its ass to the gym and lift weights; it takes a truly creative individual to extemporaneously choose words that will impress upon the listener a sense of urgency, inspiring wonder. Stringing those words along into a sentence requires masterful skills attained only after years of practice. I don't think Eddie has years to practice. Not with so many emotions working against him, and in my favor.

Friday, November 29

Friday night's the earliest we can see Bobby without arousing too much suspicion. Bobby wants to do it in a hotel, but I refuse. I've already established that if Eddie's getting involved, then operations run on my terms.

What makes it easier to convince him to agree to my terms is my leverage. Mrs. D has seen mysterious charges pop up on her husband's credit card statements. She and Bobby might even have a joint checking account. At the very least, she manages the family's finances independent of Bobby's input. He's had to explain away those charges, and I can't imagine he'd like to explain away something heavier, like infidelity, or homosexuality, or statutory rape. He will do as I say. He doesn't have a choice.

It's really not a big deal. Mrs. D is visiting her out-of-state parents for the weekend, so there's little risk of getting caught. Even if we do get caught, the worst that can happen is she takes it personally and fails me at the end of the year. Oh, no.

Their house is a bungalow with vines creeping up the walls. An older home built well. Neighbors won't hear a peep through these walls. The driveway is only wide enough for one car, but that's okay because Bobby has picked us up in his Volvo.

Before anyone gets undressed, Bobby fetches Shirley Temples for us. In all good conscience, he can't serve alcohol to minors.

"We're already here. Bring out the good stuff or we're leaving."

He caves and pours liquid from an expensive looking glass

bottle sitting on a shelf.

"Give me the Shirleys back, then. You can't mix this stuff."

Eddie looks concerned, but I assure him that we're all right to drink because we saw him pour the drink. The Shirley Temples contain no contaminants. Eddie's shoulders relax after a second sip.

"We didn't even toast," I complain. "Get yourself a drink so we can toast."

Bobby reluctantly pours himself a glass and does as he's told. The advantages of being young are incredible. I almost feel sorry for those video game addicts who can't pull away from their dungeons and socialize in the real world. If they want to leave their potential untapped, squandering their youth away in obscurity, then that's their problem.

After a few sips, Bobby leads us to his daughter's bedroom. A nursery drowning in pink. Little Sandra's belly slowly rises and falls with each breath.

"See? She's sleeping. We need to keep it down."

"Yes," Eddie whispers. "Quiet."

"I can't get aroused if I'm thinking about babies, unlike some people," I say, glaring at Bobby. Then I close the baby's bedroom door.

□□□

Sam Adams joins the party too, but only because Bobby won't pour more hard liquor. If we're going to try liquor, we should do it before beer, he says. (Still no idea what that liquor was, but it burned my throat.) The three of us have reached our limits. Careful consideration of noise level? What a joke. The moaning, thumping and screaming helped to rejuvenate this sorry bungalow. These bedroom walls have longed to see fresh faces; they've grown tired of watching Mrs. D take it doggy style. Yes, even inanimate objects have their limits.

Eddie and Bobby are sprawled on the bed, drunk and spent. Apparently Eddie doesn't know his limit, and I suspect he'll be vomiting shortly. Surely Bobby knows what he can handle, but when an opportunity like this comes along, why not go overboard? I mean, you only live once, right? If those young kids who make you feel like you'll live forever–if they solicit you for a fun night, you do not say No, under any circumstances. I feel like such a cheap fuck. I could have asked for more.

I wander the house, fully clothed just in case I need to break away, and search for incriminating evidence, because no matter how many endorphins are released, I keep legalities on the back burner. The legal field has opened up so many opportunities and loop holes, it's amazing.

I look around their cluttered craftsman house and can't focus on any one item or drawer, so I start with the computer, the family computer, because Bobby uses a MacBook Air and I'm almost positive that it's locked. Then again, maybe not. He's careless.

The home computer is not locked, but I do have to select a user. I go in under Bobby's name, which prompts me for a password, so I select Admin instead.

Doesn't matter how I get in, as long as I do.

I hear a whine upstairs and decide that there's no time to search history or files or pictures, so I navigate the settings until I spot the IP address of this individual computer. Using a pen and a sticky note, I write down the IP address and stuff it into my underwear. Onto another sticky note I jot a short paragraph and then locate a math textbook on the coffee table. The sticky note goes on the page for Monday's lesson plan. I guess paying attention during class has helped quite a bit.

A stream can be heard hitting water. Someone awake, peeing. I head upstairs.

In the bedroom, Bobby lies unconscious.

Eddie.

In the bathroom, Eddie's gagging (in the wrong way), and I ruffle his hair, praising him for drinking. For stepping out of his comfort zone. Positive reinforcement, yes. He'll do it again, now that he's had a taste. How many people can say their first time was a threesome? He should thank me for making him so incredibly interesting, because if a person I hated opened a conversation with those bragging rights, I'd listen all the way til the end.

It's 1:06 a.m. Shit.

I pull Eddie up by the hair and make him rinse off. I almost want to yell at him to get dressed, but I can't wake Bobby. I steal a pair of Bobby's light shorts that are easy to slip on and then tell Eddie to give me his jeans. I'll carry them. No need for a shirt or underwear–just the jacket. He steps clumsily. With each step, it's as if he's trying to add as many pounds per square inch as possible. I sit him down and slap him into shape. "Wait here and be quiet," I say. His head lolls to the side.

Bobby's still snoozing away, unperturbed. For the first time all evening, I notice a cat sneak out from under a dresser. Funny. I fully expected Mrs. D to have not just one cat, but a dozen. My ability to read people could use some fine tuning. It's unacceptable to be so far off the mark. At least I correctly guessed the species of pet.

Anyway, I snap a picture of Bobby's naked body for good measure. If he hasn't learned by now, then that's too bad for him. Whatever happens to him, he deserves it.

A sticky note goes onto his hands. Every household should have Post-Its, that's what I believe. The message reads: "Left early. Enjoy your crabs." Just fucking with him.

A whining sound. Is that really the baby? I open the nursery door and there's Little Sandra, wiggling around in the crib.

It's risky, but I can't help myself. I tower over the baby, saying Coochie Coo and tickling her chin until she smiles. Those soft cheeks and round eyes. She's younger than me. Tonight, I thought the power belonged to me, when it actually belonged to her. She hasn't even done anything with her life, and yet she gets all the attention. Well, if attention is what she wants, she can have it.

The baby smiles and touches me. Her entire hand wraps around half of my index finger. Stupid little bitch in training, trying to control people before she can even talk. Using my free hand, I pinch the baby on the arm really, really hard, careful not to break the skin. Little Sandra's face contorts into something ugly, and her eyes fill with hurt. The wailing begins, and I can't help but laugh at the helpless piece of shit. I reach down and whisper into her ear, "You are a worthless little cunt."

Then I bail, closing the door behind me.

I grab Eddie by his arm and say to him, "Good job tonight."

With his arm over my shoulder, we wobble out the front door and slide into the Mercedes. The driver doesn't turn on the headlights until we reach a stop sign. I pull my phone out and thank Alyssa for her service. She did me a huge favor, and on Sunday I'll follow through with my end of the deal. I have to earn Kristen's trust somehow.

Sunday, December 1

Sunday used to be the day of rest for me, but now I can't even leave my shirt untucked. I'm wearing an Oxford shirt under a vest, khaki pants, my dad's old brown moccasins and a belt that I snatched from the clearance rack.

Kristen McNicky takes her religion very seriously, and until I dig under her skin, so do I. The hard part's over though, because she's sitting in the back row with me. Mom's across the aisle and in a different row. Between Kristen and me, the love for Christ flows powerfully, igniting my goodwill and compassion, Hallelujah. During Study Hall on Friday, I memorized one of the Psalms. They all ring with beauty, like poems, but whoever wrote them sterilized the whole bunch. At least the destruction in Revelation keeps you turning the page.

So here she is, sitting next to me, crossing and uncrossing her legs like she has to pee. Does she have to use the bathroom? Who knows? The baggie in my pocket makes too much noise during this quiet service, so I'm not free to shuffle my legs around like she can. Yet another thing she can do that I cannot. That needs to be reversed.

"I have to use the bathroom," I say.

"Me too, actually," she whispers.

Too easy.

Being close to the back, we distract few people as we bound around the faux pillars and the teak wood. I turn around once more, just to look at all the zombies waiting for an amen. The pastor looks up, looks down. Looks up again, at me. I turn around. What's he going to do? Send me to Hell? Does it upset him that I won't be hypnotized by his drivel?

Kristen and I head to the bathrooms. Whoever finishes first (me) will wait at the water fountain. I stare in the mirror and plan what I'm going to say while tracking the time. I fully expect her to take at least three times as long, but when I step out, she's the one tapping her foot.

"You were fast," I say.

"You were slow."

She was so fast, in fact, that she didn't even use the electric dryer. I know that because she's drying her hands on her dress. For someone who can do no wrong, she's certainly skating on the edge.

"You look out of it today," I say.

"I'm just pissed off. Grounded."

"Because of Halloween?"

"Yeah."

"You didn't even do anything wrong. You weren't even drinking."

"Tell that to my dad. He says that my behavior lately has been unladylike. That God's children don't behave like I do."

"That must be hurtful, you being one of God's children and all."

She squints and looks at my face as if there's watercolor paint on my nose.

"Honor thy Father and thy Mother and thy day will be long in the land, isn't that how it goes?"

"Yes. I'm very impressed. I didn't even know you were a Christian."

"It's how I was raised," I gloat. "My mom took me to a different church when I was younger, but the lessons are all the same wherever you go."

Kristen bends down and takes a sip from the water fountain, bounces back up and ties her hair in a ponytail using a band pulled from thin air. Women baffle me sometimes. She just pulled that hair band out of nowhere. I should have noticed.

We exchange our personal backgrounds. She apologizes for never having noticed me when we were in grade school, because hey, we've only been going to the same schools since we were five. She was going to learn my name eventually, right? Right. She had eighteen years to catch on, but instead of taking responsibility for her intentional avoidance, she feigns ignorance, which is much more hurtful. Then again, she could be telling the truth.

The crowd inside says, "Amen."

"Is service over?"

"Sounds like it," Kristen says.

"I don't want it to be over. I like talking to you."

"Aw, thanks. I feel the same way."

"Listen, I don't want to bother you at school–because I know you're very popular and all that–"

"You can talk to me anytime," she assures me.

This is a lie. Kind of like how friends you haven't seen in a long time say they want to hang out again sometime soon, but two months later? Not another word. Six months later and still nothing. Off course, instead of "want" they use "should." But Kristen must feel sorry for me by now, so maybe she'll say yes. I did everything short of shedding a tear, so she has to say yes. Nietzsche said something along those lines, about Christians and sympathy.

"Really? Anytime?"

"Anytime!"

"How about after school one day?"

"If I'm not still grounded, then sure."

Mass lets out and the men are leaving ahead of their wives, eager to watch the game all afternoon while their wives cook and clean. That's the way these religious nuts like it. Like we're still in 1956.

Kristen's dad strays from the crowd, ostensibly to use the bathroom, and locates us instead. He immediately asks about me.

"He's a friend from school, Dad." She puts her hands on her hips and harrumphs, as if we're in a cheesy sitcom. "I can talk to friends at church, can't I?" I look him dead in the eye and he nods. "He seems like a good egg." He introduces himself with a handshake.

Pleasantries are exhausting, but I have to put in the effort. Once I have his initial approval, snaking my way into her life will be a breeze. I quote a message from today's sermon to solidify his trust in me, and next thing you know, Kristen has to pull her dad away from me.

"Dad! Mom's waiting in the car!"

"Oh, okay dear," he gruffs, and then turns to me. "You're a good egg. Why don't you come over for dinner one of these days? Martha would love a new boy who isn't like that Connor kid. Is he one of your friends too? Connor?"

"Dad."

"All right, all right." He smiles once more at me and waddles off, obviously pleased with himself.

I pull a piece of paper from my pocket and cross an item off the list. All in a day's work.

□□□

The rest of the afternoon Mom spends clipping coupons. Not that she'll buy half the items she can save money on, but she says the process relaxes her. Part of a routine that she can grow with during her recovery. It also keeps her mind off the bottle until a beer coupon sprouts from the pile and tempts her. She claims to throw those away.

Lately, she's even been talking about taking on a job. The fear of being cut off from government aid discourages her, but she talks about taking responsibility and other garbage. Oh, oh. She doesn't want to rely on anyone. She wants to take care of me all by herself.

The bitch doesn't realize that I won't have to live under her roof much longer, especially now that my grades have been improving. (The first report card is abysmal, but in the past. More inspiring to think of that as rock bottom, from which I can only go up.)

All this work on self-improvement makes me itchy. Some-body should at least be brought down if this household is going up. Luckily, I have Kristen and Eddie in my palms. They aren't on the back burner quite yet. And Mom, being an imp, really thinks she's doing good by me with her stupid rituals. That way lies madness.

Does she honestly think she can change everything now? Did my dad really have to brutally assault me before she got a clue? Taking so long to arrive at such a realization—an epiphany, a new lease on life—can't be anything but a crime. It's a crime that I've had to suffer for this long. I'd've been better off in foster care.

For heaven's sake, Alyssa takes better care of me.

And emotional support? Please. Mom's soused out of her mind half the time. I don't know what she's learning in church, but those sermons' messages sound a lot different to me than they do to her. Emotional and spiritual support—I can get those from friends. And—okay, I'll stop. Can't keep a straight face. Since Friday night, I've been blowing off Eddie and Bobby, and not in the way they appreciate. They've been bombing my phone with text messages all weekend.

First, Bobby has been sending texts and voice mails detailing his fury. I outed him, he says. The fault lies with him, however, and he's too stupid to realize that. He's had more than thirty years to learn how to play the game of life, and he still hasn't. Today, at thirty-seven years old, he's immature and irresponsible. Someone ought to put a leash on him. He should divorce his wife and marry me.

Eddie's no better, sadly. I mean, he does no better for his own well-being. I don't care what he does for himself. I just wish he'd take a hint and leave me alone for a weekend, but he thinks boyfriends must communicate every goddamn day. Where's the fun in that, exactly? You learn everything about a person in two months and then you're sick of each other, looking for fresh material before the six-month anniversary.

This is for his own good, I'll tell him. Leave me alone for a weekend so I can focus on my other subjects, I'll tell him. What about Friday night? He'll ask me. I'll shrug and say yeah, so what. Be happy I got you a threesome and spruced up your lame existence. Because you haven't been doing much for me lately. And then he'll retort with a list (guessing) of all the times he's visited and tutored, and I'll point out that that very obsession just might be the reason I don't want to see him for a weekend. You're suffocating me! Boy do I love Hollywood for all these clichs.

Without a doubt, he'll eat my every word. He'll lap at it like the dog he is. I have too much control over him. He may know that, but he's powerless to stop it. He won't cheat, but he'll fear that I will. Like, if I don't talk to you for one day, I'm cheating. As if that's an awful thing. I cheat on Mrs. D's quizzes because Eddie's a terrible tutor, always trying to arouse me when time is limited. It's like I don't have any choice but to cheat, lest I attend summer school.

Suddenly, Eddie surprises me. Sitting here in front of the TV, watching a Lifetime movie so that I can better relate to the women in my life, I receive a lewd picture of Eddie. Then another, with him naked and showing his face. Full body fun. The caption reads, "I miss you so much. Let me come over there." Those eyes are so wanting, so needing; they remind me of myself and my own needs. The reason I decided to become the Prom King this school year.

I check my email. Two sex tapes. They run on for several minutes, no holds barred. He bared all, and rather than excite me they intrigue me. I have so many new options, I don't know what to do first.

Discipline comes first. Take data, come up with a plan, execute. Everyone does this, but with varying roadblocks. Some take too much data and are paralyzed into inaction. Some come up with a plan but then come up with another plan (and then another). Some execute incorrectly because their data is flawed. Some can't take emotions out of the equation and go through the process correctly, but not fast enough to accomplish anything. Not me. I have no idea what that's like. When I set my mind to something, I follow through. Emotions only lead to disaster, as Eddie so perfectly exemplifies.

I turn off the Lifetime movie and mull over ideas. By tomorrow, my approach must be bulletproof. I have to act like nothing's wrong, just like everyone else.

We're all pretending.

Monday, December 2

A new week of school.

Mrs. Desmond returns quizzes. I barely passed. Logarithmic functions can go fuck themselves. She gives me a stern look as she walks by. Not a look of conviction, but one of suspicion. I'll be talking to her in the future. If not today, then maybe tomorrow. She can go fuck herself too.

In English, Mr. K talks about Tony Morrison's *Beloved*, and I'm amazed at the way that it opens. Any woman who can cut the throat of her own daughter gets a star in my book.

It's easy to absorb these details, because Clint's not sitting next to me. Mr. K says that he's transferred to a different English class. "Scheduling conflicts," he calls them. Yeah, right.

Clint's not at our table during lunch, either. I doubt he even has the same lunch period anymore, but I read on Facebook that he's sitting with the pot-smoking musician want-to-bes. A social connector like Clint must stay well lubricated as new contacts reach out to him, and his huge ego won't let him decline invitations. He'll have to try everything once, or else he'll kick himself for it later. I've seen his type in countless movies. He likes comfort and stability, just like a Taurus (thanks, Facebook, for the useless information).

Zack's missing too. Supposedly he's under serious pressure to conform after the Halloween party. Even his pushover mother couldn't let that one slide. If he's lucky, he'll be a go-go boy at a seedy Montreal nightclub in two years, tops. The fast, easy money will tie him over for a while, but then he'll go broke at twenty-one, when he buys Stolichnaya wholesale. Alcoholism will then take over, so either his parents will intervene or he'll just die.

Alternatively, he could join the military, as a kind of detox. Ah, the military. Zack will fit right in, being a brainless monkey and all. In society's mind, that's an example of turning one's life around. When he returns, everyone will laud his efforts, calling him brave, so I guess Zack will be fine no matter what he does. Michael Yulgov will do something similar, but there's hope for him. He possesses a certain charm that only a second generation child has. Perhaps that's why I haven't used him yet. His true colors will come out soon enough.

Eddie, on the other hand, needs to go. Because here on the hallway floor with the other rejects who can't mold themselves into any particular table identity, he's bitching me out for ignoring him all weekend.

He's so pathetic. Talking about how sensitive he is, how much it hurt, and, oh my–he's no longer a virgin! His thoughts are so scrambled and his emotions so frantic, he doesn't know if he should be proud or ashamed. He wants to undo everything and have another chance, but he won't get it. No one ever gave me a second chance. He can figure things out on his own.

Out of the grace of my heart, I will give him something to remember. If he's confused now, he won't know what to do with himself once I cross a few items off my to-do list. I already have the photo and video evidence, so all I have to do is choose the delivery.

With this task, I'm not even trying to become Prom King. This is just for fun.

Tuesday, December 3

Eddie thinks I haven't responded to his texts because I left my phone at the Desmonds'. That's the lie I fed him, and now he's worried that his lurid content has fallen into the wrong hands. Mrs. D's.

At least his fears take some of the heat off of me. Oh, sure, Eddie. If I'd had my phone, I would have replied, really! Oops. Too late. The pictures and videos are "out there" now. (By "out there" I mean that my email account is accessible on my phone, because I don't lock anything. Nothing is guarded by password, so if it were to fall into the wrong hands, then I'd have a real problem. Transparency begets trust–that was my thinking, and it's why my Facebook account is visible to the public.)

Here in my bedroom, I'm touching up the images and videos in a free editor. Now that Eddie truly believes me, I can proceed. Maybe there's a chance that everything will trace back to me, but the risk is thrilling. I haven't felt this excited in a while.

This stupid town will have a Merry Christmas with the gift I am about to send around. Superimposing the Desmonds' IP address onto the footage is easier than I thought. A quick Internet search resulted in several resources, so I chose the second result. Done. It gets the work done.

Next, I upload the videos to all the tube sites, using a new screen name for each one. (I already have several email accounts set up for the sole purpose of registering new accounts on tube sites.) I don't know how to do much else, so planting the seeds will suffice for now. Horny pervs all over the world live for the thrill of finding these.

If I had more technical savvy, I'd upload them remotely, or something. I don't know. Whatever they do in the movies. There's a learning curve, sure. Sometimes you have to pull the trigger even if you feel unprepared. Fire it off and you may be surprised at what you accomplish.

But that in no way means do shoddy work. For all the enjoyment I derive from this, I have a few safety measures to ensure my liberties stay intact. (To Eddie's credit, there is some enjoyment to be derived from the videos. He included his face and body in the frame, and the lighting hits him just right. And he's not wearing glasses, so he looks good.)

Once all the seeds have been planted, I shut down my computer and lie on my back. If I'm lucky, then not only will I be cleared of any wrongdoing, but I won't even be suspected. Ideally, the whole school will stumble upon the footage and Principal Snow will have a few words with the school. Eddie's parents will know too, from their sources. It'd be funny if they watch the whole video, just to see if their baby knows how to finish.

Although control would be nice, I can't have all of it and expect to avoid detection. Unfortunately, now that I've sent it out, cyberspace controls how far Eddie Fischer's private collection travels. That ticks me off a little.

Wednesday, December 4

Kristen McNicky is nowhere to be found during lunch. I did one sweep through the cafeteria before Eddie caught up with me. And then another after I dragged him with me to Mrs. D's classroom to "pick up" my cell phone. He waited in the hallway. When I came out with my cell phone, his skin blanched.

To relieve him, I dragged him away from the scene by his collar and to the cafeteria, where we were served steamed broccoli and fried rice, like this is fucking China King. Alyssa might've been pleased, but I certainly wasn't. I had to pretend, though, because showing my sturdy exterior to Eddie means that he can take comfort in leaning on me when those moments of weakness diminish his judgment.

Now we're sitting on the floor in the hallway (again) and Eddie's being more touchy feely than I'm used to. He almost doesn't care who sees us. Then again, no one wants to look down at the peons who sit on the floor in the hallway, those fringe students who can't be categorized.

I worked so hard during the first two weeks of school to land my spot at the cool kids' table, only to be dragged down by this dweeb. He's so infuriating, I'm tempted to take this spork and stab him in the eye.

"Go ahead," Eddie says. "Just look at them. No one can see." He puts an arm around my shoulder. I pinch his hand and peel it off.

"Do you really think that's a good idea? I mean, look where we are. I can't get horny in public."

"Come on, you'll like it."

"I don't want to wait until after school to relieve myself. I'm telling you, this video is gonna be hot, all because you're in it."

"I know," Eddie says. "If you want, you can relieve yourself here. I know how much you like having sex in public places. In bathrooms."

I can't tell if Eddie is pulling my leg, but he's being too specific for a coincidence. I face him directly for the first time since we sat down, pinch his cheeks so that his mouth deflates through his lips and then ask him where he heard that.

"Mr. D told me," he says.

"His name is Bobby. Bobby. Keep calling him Mr. D and we're going to get in trouble. He sounds like an adult when you put it that way. Just plain creepy." "But isn't he? I thought you liked it that way. He told me you did."

"Okay, but that was back then. Now, I only have eyes for you." I sigh and attempt to add more heft to my voice. A watery tone or a trembling lip will suffice. At the same time, I'm conscious of the steamed broccoli or fried rice that might be in my teeth, so I can't go all-out. "I got that out of my system last -weekend. Over it. You're all that matters to me now. You know that."

Eddie's not paying attention to the environment, despite the crowd of students walking in our direction, students who will no doubt say something when they notice our faces so close together. From where they stand, they do not have to literally look down at us. They see us straight ahead, the brick backdrop framing us well enough for a pamphlet photo. An LGBT pamphlet.

"Do you really mean that?" He's so pathetic and lovestruck. Blinded. He can't see what's in his current environment, so he definitely won't see my betrayal coming. I have him properly hooked, but I need a few finishing touches to assuage upcoming suspicions.

"I do," I say, and lean in to kiss him with my eyes open. His eyes are closed. Guess he'll never know.

The group of students walks right past us, either because

they didn't notice us or because they felt uncomfortable by what they just witnessed.

Thursday, December 12

Alyssa keeps telling me to relax, that Clint is just a big oaf who likes comfort and stability. "And if he wants stability, he can have it with the new crowd he's with. I'm friends with all of them."

"Let me see," I say. "He unfriended me."

"Here, look."

Sure enough, foreign-looking names populate Clint's time line of recent activity. "He's friends with–how do you pronounce that? That's his last name?" It reads: Pichaironnarong-songkram.

"How the hell should I know? Just because we're both Asian doesn't mean we speak the same language. He's a Thai boy."

"Doesn't he have a nickname? It just looks impossible to pronounce."

"He goes by Pit," Alyssa says. "I've seen him hang out with computer people. Whatever. One of those nerds. Stereotype! Maybe Clint has nothing against you. Maybe he's just bored with you."

"That's a possibility," I groan. "Misty has been introducing him to tons of Japanese cartoons. He probably has yellow fever."

"Then it's only a matter of time before he finds himself a nice Thai woman. Then he'll move there and be like all the other sex-pats. Yucky white guys who move there to screw teenage girls."

I can't help but laugh. Alyssa's the only one who understands my humor. She knows how to make me laugh without trying, or at least she pretends to not try. Could be an effortless act, in which case I say: Bravo.

"May I?" I gesture toward Alyssa's laptop.

"You wanna stalk some people? Be my guest."

"Thanks."

Alyssa walks out of her bedroom and closes the door behind her, as if she's daring me to do something on her laptop. I can't tell if she's bluffing or if she's actually that careless, but I don't take the risk. Cameras might be training their focus on me, cameras hidden throughout the room–microscopic, almost invisible cameras. Her daddy can afford them, certainly. I play it safe and venture no further than the Facebook domain until she returns with two bowls of butterscotch ice cream.

"Thanks," I say again.

"You're welcome." Alyssa sits on the bed Indian style and straightens her spine before spooning up the first bite. "You'll have to watch your back soon enough. Remember? Two months ago you couldn't gain weight, and now you have gained so much muscle, I actually wanna fuck you."

"Oh boy, don't tempt me."

"We can, like, do cardio together." A brownish glob of ice cream remains on her lips after a few more spoonfuls. Some of it dribbles down to her chin, and she fingers it back into her mouth while keeping her eyes trained firmly on me. "How does that sound?"

"I'll have to do something. I don't want to turn into a total meat head. I could use some toning down."

"But remember: the Prom King isn't usually toned down. The Prom King is a stereotype, just like Pit is a stereotype. So the Prom King is a football player. He gets to date and screw the most popular girls in school, and he's familiar with most students on a first-name basis. I'm not sure if you fit any of that criteria."

"Those criteria."

"*Puk gai, lah,*" Alyssa scoffs. "Face it, you'll never win. Even with Connor out of football, remember that Zack took his place. Both of them will be playing either tennis or lacrosse.

Do you really think you can compete with them physically?"

"You have a point there," I say, looking away from the laptop. I walk to the bed and sit next to her with my bowl of butterscotch ice cream. "You must do a lot of cardio to stay so skinny. How do you eat so much junk food and stay in shape?"

"Well, I have a giant Buddha statue in my closet. First, I meditate in front of him. This happens every morning before I even think about breakfast. If I believe I will become skinny, then I will."

"Wow, what a load of bullshit."

"I know, right?" Alyssa scoffs. "Nah, the truth is that I fuck the Buddha statue. Burns far more calories and keeps me happy. Buddha never says no. He doesn't believe in past or future; he only thinks about pleasing me in the present."

We both laugh at this. Alyssa nonchalantly airplanes a spoon of her ice cream into my mouth, and I do the same for her.

"No, but seriously," Alyssa says, "there's a lot of sex involved. You burn a lot of calories that way. Maybe you should put more effort into that with your boyfriend. Eddie Fischer?"

"How did you know?" I gasp, widening my eyes and covering my mouth.

"One of my friends saw you and him kissing during lunch. How cute is that?"

"Word gets around," I say.

"Sure, sure. And, like I said earlier, do you think the Prom King is a, um, homosexual? No, it never happens. I don't know what kind of movies you watch, but if you want that title, you'll have to attend a gay prom somewhere. They're all over the place now. Have you even thought of who your date is going to be?"

"Probably you, or maybe Kristen or one of the other girls." I shrug. "Any girl who isn't a total beast."

"I'd be honored," Alyssa says. "Maybe we can win Prom King and Queen together. I don't think Kristen will win this year."

"Why's that?" I say, stirring the goop around in my bowl.

I've lost my appetite.

"Well, she's not exactly Prom Queen material now, if you catch my drift. Or haven't you heard?"

"What?"

"She's hooked on weed!" Alyssa jumps and bounces on the bed, having her own Eureka moment while almost spilling the goopy ice cream on the sheets.

"Our plan worked!"

"Our plan almost got me killed. That was really sketchy, meeting a drug dealer at the city library. I think you owe me."

"Patience. The real pleasure will come when she starts hanging with the stoners. Eventually, her dad will ground her so that she won't be attending any more social functions or extracurriculars that don't involve praising Jesus. Then, when that's too stressful, she'll try harder drugs. No Prom Queen I ever met has meth teeth. None."

"You have a point there. She's pretty much out of the picture."

"But you are right about one thing: I think I owe you." She gets on all fours and brushes her hands through my hair, her breath meeting my ear.

"Oh, come on."

"You come on! How do you know you're gay if you've never tried a girl before? I'm the perfect girl to try out your skills."

"I'm not really into Asians."

"Oh, fuck you."

"But I do like to try new things. So it is I who will be fucking you."

We rip our clothes off and it takes a while for me to get hard. My eyes remain closed most of the time. I have to think about other things. I put my hand over her mouth so she doesn't squeak like the Asians in the movies.

After we finish, she falls asleep and I cover her naked body with her now-soiled 800-thread count sheets, because her dad can't walk in and see her exposed. The only reason I'm allowed to hang out with her is because her father believes that I am gay (which I am, really). No one will believe that I had sex with Alyssa Zaianassey if I tell them.

With my new information on Clint and Kristen, I feel confident enough to face the day tomorrow, athletic shortcomings be damned. I'll sit with new people at lunch, hop around from table to table. People have to familiarize themselves with me and my story, and then they'll be more likely to vote for me. I descend the Brazilian redwood staircase, holding the exotic wood railing. I never really noticed the details in this mansion before, but it does look very Singaporean. Maybe I know that now because I've been inside Miss Singapore.

Dropping my bowl and spoon into the sink, I acknowledge the Filipina maid and head to the front closet, where she stored my coat. I'm glad I brought a coat and not a jacket, because a snowflake lands on my nose. In the distance, the driver exits the vehicle and positions himself so that he's facing me with his hands intertwined behind his back. I can't see his hands, but that's how they have to be, according to all the movies I've seen. The driver is a stereotype.

He's wearing a coat, too. I am not alone.

He hits the gas and neither of us says a word, as usual.

Sunday, December 15

Sunday comes and goes. I don't attend mass, because Kristen's already hooked on the cannabis and it's only a matter of time before her father disowns her.

My work is done. The rest will take care of itself.

Wednesday, December 25

Christmas comes and goes. Mom bought me a novel I never asked for, and that's all. No talk about my dad coming back; it's obvious that he won't. So it's just us sitting around the tinseled tree, reminiscing about past Christmases, looking forward to better ones.

She suggests that we move on from Christmas and think about the New Year. I ask her what her resolution is and she says it's to be a better mother to me. It's hard not to puke, but I stifle my gag.

She asks me about my New Year's resolution and I tell her that I want to become the Prom King.

"What a lofty goal," she says. That bitch.

Eddie wanted to spend Christmas with us but I basically told him to fuck off. He has his family and I have mine. Haven't we spent enough time together? Does he really have to take over my holidays too? I didn't tell him that. I only blamed my mother, saying that it was her wish that Christmas Day be celebrated without guests. Family members only.

Eddie agreed and said that that sounded fair.

Thursday, January 2

Eddie's restlessness annoys the shit out of me. Totally insatiable. What started off as a neurotic, paranoid personality has evolved or devolved into something ugly that he should have been up front about on our first date.

It's sickening, being pulled into the same direction for so long. There's no magnetism other than the kind he has created between us. I detect nothing, and yet I can't eschew him without blowing my cover.

However, I get lucky. In the first week of the New Year, Eddie's called into Principal Snow's office and that can only mean one thing. The leaked videos. Alyssa tells me on the ride home.

"He's going to call you any second now," she says.

"Yeah."

Now I'm sitting in the living room, refusing to touch homework until Eddie calls me. When he does, I listen to him whine and complain–on the verge of tears–about how that video got out. I tell him that it's not my fault. Robert "Hot Dad" Desmond stumbled upon my missing phone in his house, when we had a threesome. That's what I tell Eddie.

Reinforcement is so important when dealing with needy people. He deserves embarrassment for being so foolish. Not my problem he's irresponsible. The fact that I once mentioned the phone being out of my possession really does help my story.

"What am I gonna do?" He's crying now.

"Just relax. It's not that bad. Lots of guys do it and they move on just fine."

"I won't move on just fine," he screams. I pull the phone from my ear and kind-of listen. "They called my parents. My dad's gonna kill me and I won't be able to look at my mom in the face ever again. And school–I can't show my face there. Everyone knows, Jude. Every single person knows."

Offering him a place to stay so he can escape it all–that would be counterproductive. That's what he wants from me, but I skate around the topic. "Well, just breathe–hey, breathe."

Mom walks through the front door carrying groceries, so I stand up and walk upstairs, shutting the door behind me.

"Breathe, Ed. I'm right here. It's not the end of the world."

"Yes, it is."

A few minutes go by, and because Eddie enjoys being unreasonably dramatic, I sever the line, citing homework as my excuse. There's just so much to do in so little time! Click.

Mom calls for me to help her put the groceries away. Like a good son, I obey.

ㅁㅁㅁ

Dodging Eddie's calls for help proves to be an aggravating challenge. I give him just enough attention to show that he's still my boyfriend, but avoid PDA altogether. He has to stay half a foot away from me when walking in the halls. The distance helps you collect your thoughts so that you may think before you speak, I tell him. He eats it, nodding like a petulant child.

The sadness still lingers in his eyes, those eyes that scan the hallway. He wants to cower behind me, and at times, I let him. High school can be tough. I spot Misty and Clint holding hands in the science hallway. She hasn't changed her hideous tie-dye style yet, and Clint still dresses like a house painter. Good for them. They've lasted, what, three months now? In high school time, that's commendable.

They walk into the computer lab and do a bowing gesture in front of a short brown boy. Right, it's Pit. If these Asians don't take over the world in population, or with their fucked up names, then they will do so by hacking the world's computer network or database. Does the world have a centralized one? Oh, whatever. They'll take over the Internet. I've heard of hackers in India that can be hired for $5 an hour. Yeah, they'll take over one way or another, which is why Clint and Misty are converting to Yellowism and learning Yellow People customs, such as the ridiculous bowing gestures.

Well, I hang out with Alyssa Zaianassey, who is rich and half white, half yellow. I'm on that side of the fence too, see. I'll adjust my expectations once high school is over, maybe take some Mandarin classes in college.

Speaking of college, I sent a few applications out over the break. A little late, but not too late. They expect a glut of mail around this time, so I'm still a contender for the crummy state schools whose bars have been lowering year after year.

The myth of the straight-A student getting into school is over. Now, the straight-A student gets accepted to a wider range of schools, whereas the C-student gets in somewhere. Most likely a state school, and a community college at the very least. In fact, plenty of straight-A students are matriculating into community college curricula. That's just economics, which they will learn in their first two semesters when they take classes on economics.

How silly it is to wait until college to learn. Learning is lifelong, but apparently we need school systems to charge us up the ass before they can grace us with that realization. Not that I've fallen for it, because I do my own research. I keep up with trends and study human behavior constantly.

Additionally, I study outside of facts, because facts are boring. I can look up any fact on the Internet. Sorry, academics, but it's true.

That's okay. I'll play the game everyone wants me to play and try my hand at college. In the meantime, I have to graduate from high school first. I'd like to leave a lasting impression, which was my goal at the beginning of the school year.

I won't let Misty or Zack or Alyssa or Eddie or Principal Snow or Mrs. D or anyone stop me from achieving what I set out to do. That's the kind of perseverance that no institution can teach you; the hunger must reside within.

After a long day of struggling to stay awake during my new classes, and at the same time not becoming overstimulated by Eddie's drama, I plop down on the couch and take a long nap.

Upon waking, my phone buzzes and I almost want to slam it against the wall, it's so annoying. I swipe the screen and flick through the messages detailing news that I did not see coming.

Eddie committed suicide.

Part 2

Explaining the suicide to Mom sounded like a bad idea in my head until I remembered that she knew he and I were dating. Now she knows, and she's crying about it.

"He was such a sweet boy!"

"Yes, he was."

"Why would he do something like that?"

"I don't know, ma." I drop my voice really low so she knows I am sad.

Tomorrow will not be a better day.

Friday, January 3

Of course the whole day is going to suck now that I have to hear another speech by Principal Snow. That's right. Once again, every student is dragged from their classes and forced to sit through yet another school play–I mean ceremony.

Clint and Misty greet me at the top bleacher and bow their heads solemnly, as if to say that despite our differences, they want to put that in the past, even for just one day. Me, I don't believe in forgiveness. I tell them to fuck off and sit next to their Thai friend, Pit.

Zack Eldin, instead of rushing to the top row to find a good seat, hugs the Royal Ocelot mascot. That's right. For this ceremony, someone went through the actual thought process of considering to wear a costume. As if the school hasn't been grieving enough already. How dare he. Or should I say she?

The Royal Ocelot has removed its fuzzy purple head, revealing a female student. From where I'm sitting she looks like any girl, but by the way she's holding Zack's hand and leaning her head on him, I figure she is Zack's sister. Yeah, that's one way to cramp your style. No wonder he never talks about his sister. What he said about her buying alcohol for the party was most likely a lie.

Now if only her social destitution could prevent him from being nominated for Prom King, we'll be in business. Or maybe everyone will see how sensitive and caring he is toward his sister; maybe it will work in his favor.

Principal Snow claims the gymnasium's center, and then speaks into the microphone.

"Students and faculty, it is with tremendous regret that I inform you of a tragedy that occurred last night. A tragedy that will haunt us for ..." Blah, blah, blah. I can't believe I have to sit through this shit. People around me are bawling and no matter how convincing an actor I may be, I can't possibly match genuine tears.

Even worse, the attention will likely shift to me, seeing as how I was dating Eddie before he offed himself. Yeah, they'll think I had something to do with it, so I already have strikes against me. I think I can prove my innocence. After all, Eddie was a free agent who acted of his own volition. Causing emotional turmoil is not a crime.

But uploading videos of an underage boy masturbating? That might be. I superimposed the Desmonds' IP address onto the footage, so that should wrangle me free of suspicion. I can hardly wait to see Mrs. D's reaction. She must be full of opinions.

Until that shit storm hits, I have nothing else to do but sit and wait. Utilizing my elevation and distance from the center of the gymnasium, I scroll through my phone and read random articles on Wikipedia.

LAMPYRIDAE

Where to start with the precious fireflies? Maybe the best place to start is at conception, or is it birth? I'll hop right into the cycle at the point of birth. Fireflies pupate nine months. Some adults hibernate for a year or more, which is strange, and that's why extinction closes in on the species as a whole. By the way, they are not even flies; technically, they are beetles.

Not all fireflies emit light, which I never knew. But there are species that emit light in the earliest phase of life, as larvae. The chemicals luciferin and luciferase combine with ATP to emit the glow we are all familiar with. Glowing like they do, you'd think they are warm, but they are in fact the opposite. Cold light, as scientists call it. Surprisingly, the light emitted from fireflies is considered by scientists to be the most efficient in the world.

Like, when a bulb lights up, it emits as much heat as it does light. (Some bulbs more, some less. I'm not going to split hairs with you on this. I'm too fascinated by the subject at hand to specify the intricacies of dead objects lacking carbon, lacking ATP.)

At this early stage, the baby firefly feeds on snails and earthworms. For the most part, fireflies are carnivorous, even if they are classified as omnivores (some do eat pollen and parts of plants). Accessibility to snails isn't an issue for the young firefly, because it hatched either underground or under the bark of a tree. Firefly light has many uses. It can ward off predators, whose taste buds might be in for a surprise if they feast upon a firefly. They oftentimes learn the hard way. But if I were an animal, I wouldn't bite into something advertised so conspicuously. Too good to be true. Porcupines ward off predators at the last moment, but fireflies tell you right from the get-go to stay away from them.

Again, not all fireflies emit light.

Additionally, these critters use light to signal one another. Scientists still can't determine how species of firefly in Southeast Asia, in large masses, can synchronize their lighting precisely (and I do mean to the millisecond). A fun way to communicate, much like we advertise businesses on the street. Shiny lights grab attention.

Mating comes to mind. There are many variations to who attracts whom, but generally a male approaches a female by light. Every so often, however, a male will attract another male. That's just nature.

Even better: females have been known to glow and attract mates, only to devour them!

Some species that don't emit any light will attract mates using pheromones. How nifty. We discovered this by putting them in blackened petri dishes and observing the results, and these blind fireflies found each other somehow. Scientists came to the conclusion that they relied solely on pheromones, but who can say for sure? There are so many mysteries unsolved.

I find it sad that they are becoming endangered. Our summer nights will lose the magic they once had, all because of light pollution. For instance, putting a road through a rural area allows cars to whir by with bright headlights that confuse fireflies by interrupting light signals. If you scramble their communication, they are less likely to mate, lay eggs, etc.

No migration takes place when one habitat is destroyed. You build your light-polluting house near a marsh and you're pretty much destroying their habitat for good. The fireflies are doomed the moment you lay pavement.

Loss of summer magic may not be a sufficient reason for you to care, fine. I can live with that. But forensic scientists rely on the production of luciferase and luciferin for, well, I don't know. Actually, nevermind. I don't care if the stupid bugs become extinct. Forensic scientists don't need to wise up one bit. Personally, I'd rather live in the Jack the Ripper era. You might think things like tracking fingerprints and analyzing hair samples would be more difficult in that era, and you would be right.

ㅁㅁㅁ

I wanted to look forward and keep walking straight ahead. That's what I wanted. The swell of students took somber, moping steps to the classrooms they'd emerged from and I was caught among them. That's where I still am–in the crowd.

I feel disconnected more than ever before. The glum chatter in the hallway tells me that Eddie will actually be missed, that his embarrassing video won't stand against him too much, even if it does serve as a cautionary tale for future students (who will fall into the traps anyway, thanks to raging hormones).

No, what troubles me about walking back to class is not that I'm alone and friendless, but that I can feel the tension and hostility wherever I go now, and– I am sideswiped, pressed against the brick wall that I once sat against with Eddie. Michael Yulgov has my shirt collar scrunched up in his fist, the other hand clenched and ready to execute. He thinks I should be frightened or threatened, but really I want to laugh at the clich.

"What did you do to him?" Mike yells. The flow of students halts, turns its attention to the drama at the brick wall.

"What did I do? This is about what he did to himself. I didn't do anything."

Last thing I need with half a school year to go is a negative reputation. This foreign fuck of ill repute is going to set me back. I'm tempted to punch Yulgov, milk this outburst for what it's worth. Everyone likes a good fight.

"Liar! You did something." He tightens his trembling fist. "What did you do?"

"Oh, you miss your tennis partner? You did a fantastic job of ignoring him when he sat at our table at the beginning of the year, remember? He didn't come out of his shell until–"

He punches me in the face. The back of my head scrapes the brick wall, and I'm worried about scabs preventing hair growth.

He's screaming at me, crying, incomprehensible. A little spittle for good measure. Nothing new here. My dad beats me way better than he does. Judging Mike's size, I can afford retaliation. A jab to the gut catches him off guard. He wheezes. When his head turns up, his eyes are filled with unabashed hatred. The crowd behind him does not cheer or leer, but they squelch in protest. They don't want a fight.

I see a second punch coming, and I fully intend to dodge.

Principal Snow slides between us on his shiny moccasins, halting the fight.

"Get back to class. Mike? Go," he says. He addresses everyone in the hall by shouting: "That's enough here. Everybody get back to class."

I protest. "Did you see what he did to me? Aren't you going to punish that monster? Look, I'm bleeding–"

"I will take care of him later. Right now, I need to see you in my office."

All I want to do is look forward and walk straight ahead. If that freak wanted to punish me, he could have done it after school sometime, because at least the cops would be able to deal with it. On school grounds, I am without rights and subjected to the principal's mercy.

On top of that, I am going to miss class. That's what I tell him as we walk to his office. I am in school to learn and study, and he's keeping me from doing what I came here to do.

"Quiet," he says. "We're about to do some learning in my office."

Snow doesn't seem to like me too much, and I'm not sure why. It's not like I've attacked him personally, even though I'd like to. Mrs. Desmond is standing next to his desk, where Snow sits, and her arms are crossed. This is a more aggressive stance than I've been led to believe she's capable of.

Snow acts like he's in charge, but I'm not buying it. Not anymore. If he were in charge, he would have prevented such a devastating tragedy from happening in the first place.

"We are very sad to be here under these circumstances today," Snow says, sighing deeply. "But the issue must be addressed."

Mrs. D remains silent.

"Exactly what issue are we talking about?" Playing dumb seems like the most logical tactic for the time being. He doesn't know as much as he thinks he does, because I've had foresight and intuition to ensure that my secrets don't leak.

"You know what I'm talking about," he says, loosening his shirt collar.

"Oh, right. I know! You're talking about the way that monster pinned me against the wall back there. Of course you are. Because that right there–that was unacceptable. Everyone saw it."

"I'm talking about your relationship with Eddie." With the office door closed, I can't hear anything in the halls. His words have double the impact, but then again, so do mine. He thinks he can intimidate me, but he can't.

"Yes, we were boyfriends. We had a lot of fun. So what? There's no law against being gay."

"No, certainly not. This school prides itself on its tolerance. You are aware of the Gay Straight Alliance we have here, aren't you?"

I nod, maintaining eye contact for a moment, but the piles of paper on Snow's desk call for my attention. Someone this sloppy shows his entire hand at once. No trumps. Folded cards with coffee stains on them. Literally. There is a Bicycle playing card trapped beneath a desk lamp, and I see the wrinkled edge. The back pattern is the standard red color. You'd think it'd be purple, as a sign of school spirit.

"Good, I'm glad we're on the same page there. This matter is not about sexual orientation." He looks at Mrs. D for a second, then back at me. "This is a matter of lewdness, Jude."

I play dumb.

"You know what I'm talking about here. You and Eddie had your hijinks at Mrs. Desmond's house, with her husband.

By hijinks I mean a sexual tryst, is that correct?"

"Yes."

"Because you left a nasty little note in her textbook. How do you speak for yourself?"

"I speak for myself proudly." My voice is confident, bold and persuasive. Conviction has led me to power before, albeit power on smaller scales, but a triumph over this pompous prick might be my crowning achievement to look back on five years from now. Hopefully a better opportunity will come along before then, but this is golden. The present. My voice sounds heavy in the cramped, confined office.

"That's such a shame. Additionally, you were failing Mrs. Desmond's class last quarter. You're barely passing now? Does that have anything to do with this aggression?"

"No."

"Then what? I'm all ears."

"You want the truth? Bobby's hot and I begged him to fuck the shit out of me. We already did it in the bathroom of a restaurant–with his baby daughter crawling on the bathroom floor. That was exciting."

Mrs. D's face drops. Too bad for her. She can't fail me out of spite. The math is either correct or it isn't. She can't be unfair.

"And when we snuck into Bobby's pad, the three of us had sex upstairs, in the master suite. It was amazing, spreading my legs in the spot where little Sandra was most likely conceived. I came so fast. And so did Eddie, once he–"

"That is enough!" Mrs. D yells. I wonder how much more I could have said. "That's enough. I won't have this anymore. There will be severe consequences for this type of behavior."

Principal Snow nods his head in agreement; he has no other choice. Personally, I like the freedom that comes with being a student, because I can take either the teacher's side or the student's side in any given confrontation. Snow must always take the teacher's side. Sad to be shackled like that. Really sad.

"Oh, please. Like you didn't know. He's been fucking boys

since before you met. I wouldn't act like this is one great big revelation if I were you, Mrs. D." I bat my eyelashes and lisp when I say her name. Teasing my prey, playing with my food. She is the peanut gallery, and cannot make any executive decisions pertaining to disciplinary measures. "That's another thing. We are boys, correct? We are underage? How unfortunate for you if any proof is released."

"You are suspended until further notice," Principal Snow snaps. My, how testy. He reacts so abrasively to facts which have not yet amounted to real threats.

"Are you sure you want to do that?" I say. "That might not end well for anyone."

"It certainly did not end well for Eddie."

"Whose fault is that? It's not my fault Eddie fell in love with Bobby and sent him that jerk-off video. Everyone has seen it. I'm surprised the cops haven't searched your house for kiddie porn yet."

Silence from them. The silence speaks for them. Always taking the easiest, most comfortable way out. Pure laziness and lack of foresight, of discipline. Even if I am severely punished for this incident, I will emerge the victor, the strongest, the most strong-willed.

"We are going to transfer you to a different math class. As for your suspension, you are not to return until Monday of the week after next. We will also be phoning your parents for a discussion."

"That's the best thing you've said all day."

"Get out. Go to class now." Snow doesn't like being butt hurt. Boo hoo.

"Bye!" I open the heavy wooden door, walk out and do an Irish click with my feet before vanishing from their sight. They don't know half the story, but at least they now know not to mess with me.

We all did some learning in that office.

□□□

Mom's all like, what do you mean you got suspended? My

response is, guess that means you're not being a better mother for the New Year, huh? That shuts her up. She knows better than to argue.

Instead, she calls my dad, who is now out of jail, and talks his ear off. The suspension has so upset her that she might redact the restraining order, endangering my life in the process, all so that we can have a semblance of family. She's crossed the line like this before, while under the influence.

Good thing I'll be out of here in six months.

For the rest of the week I'll be watching the social media concerning Eddie's death, keeping tabs on the emotional pulse of this floundering suburb. We're a progressive community, all right; we progress so quickly, we forget that we're dying, and then when death comes knocking, it's too late to change anything. Good thing I'll be out of here in six months.

Oh, she's saying that this happened because I missed a few weeks of church? She has lost it this time. She can find another crutch to help her through the boring Sunday services.

And to think that more than ninety percent of the population believe in garbage like this. No real evidence, but they believe anyway. Squabbling comes next, because theirs is the only True God. Et cetera.

Even if I'm out of here in six months, I won't ever escape people who hold inane convictions. It's easy to argue about something that only requires strong conviction. Logic falls by the wayside, and the loudest, most persuasive party wins. Sounds like excellent training for a young capitalist in a capitalist country. Appealing to those sensibilities helps to advance one's career, one's reputation.

Alyssa Zaianassey sends a text message alerting me of Edward Fischer's funeral. I'm invited because the school hasn't expelled me. Even though I looked at my phone during the assembly that Principal Snow milked for as much pity as possible. Is it any wonder that he holds so many ceremonies in the year? He's appealing to the parents' sensibilities, namely that their children are being fostered in a supportive environment.

What if ten students commit suicide in one year? Twenty?

Does Principal Snow hold assemblies for each of them, or is there a cut-off? Given that the student body will forget about Eddie two weeks after his funeral, it's safe to assume that twenty suicide assemblies in one year is impractical, wasteful and ineffective. He'd batch them all into one Friday afternoon Suicide-a-palooza and leave it at that. All schools should. Students can be numbered, just as our time can be quantified.

But I will attend his funeral, no doubt. My dark clothing will suit me well for once, and I can use the event as a study session. I can mimic facial expressions of the grieving, the addled, the deprived and depraved. It's great practice for–you guessed it–appealing to sensibilities. Anyone who remembers me getting mugged in the hall–getting tossed against a wall like that–will forgive me if I just shed a tear, tremble my lip. A sniffle works well too.

Tuesday, January 7

On my second day of suspension, I drop by the library to meet my dealer again. Kristen will be happy to receive more marijuana, which should help her through these tough times. If she's committed, she'll graduate from the kiddie stuff.

Not like she needs to. Any additional effort is overkill at this point.

The dealer, whose alias I don't know, fixates on the library's lack of security, and so do I. There are no cameras monitoring the book stacks near the back, by the reference books no one looks at because of Wikipedia.

The library works better than a private residence. The dealer doesn't need to know where I live if the shit hits the fan. One transaction and done, stay out of my life. I hand him a wad of cash in exchange for a pound. Despite Alyssa's ill feelings toward Kristen, she subsidizes a proper drug habit, ensuring that her frenemy receives the best weed in the city.

Snatch, pivot, stash, walk. I don't look back. The whole process takes less than two minutes. I dash through the snow, fat bag of weed hidden under my winter jacket, and drive off.

Upon arriving home, I tell Mom that I'll go to church this Sunday. Kristen will be there.

Thursday, January 9

Why Zack and Connor are still friends, I have no idea. If I were Connor, I would have complained about my QB position being stolen from me. Seems that they were covering for each other, because that's what bros do.

Bros have short term memory, so they've already moved on to another sport, which is great because the football thing wasn't working out. They lost more than half the games they played. I'm glad I never cheered from the bleachers.

When Michael Yulgov plays tennis, however, I will attend a few games. I will throw his concentration off, because he obviously hates me. Why not make him hate me more? Separated by a chain link fence and surrounded by spectators, he can't really hurt me.

I almost wish he would have killed himself instead. Being a second generation child in a lower middle class family must suck. He has to work twice as hard to fit in. From his mouth, the colloquialisms he imitates sound too forced and poorly accented. Why he even tries, I'll never know.

That's probably why he's mad at me. He doesn't like that I shook up our lunch period seating arrangement, effectively disbanding the clan and prompting him to find a new table. He can't stand the fact that I quickly rose in popularity from such a low rank. The unknown rank. He's been trying since middle school to play all the right sports before settling on tennis, and now he has nothing to show for his efforts except the occasional after-game milkshake. He'd argue that there's intrinsic value in playing tennis for its own sake (but he wouldn't use a word like intrinsic).

Sunday, January 12

For every time I hear the word "God" today, I should receive a dime. God, this service is unbearable. Kristen sits in the back pew with me, as usual.

Now I'm at her house, in her room. Her dad ushered me up the stairs to hopefully show that girl how to behave (as long as my positive influence shines through with the door open).

Kristen taps her foot eagerly, anticipating the bag I'm ready to give her. She's so focused on the bag, it seems, that she doesn't even talk about school or friends or church or anything.

That focus is consistent with her neglected appearance. Dark roots have overtaken much of her curly blond head, and she's given up on the powder and mascara she used to wear. The eyeliner and lip gloss remain, to ensure a whorish appearance. Her clothing is dark, too. I wonder when she changed her wardrobe. Were greys and blacks on her Christmas list?

I tell her that she can have the weed if she promises to share my Facebook posts for one month. Free of charge is almost too good to be true. She knows what I want, so I can bargain with goods I paid nothing for.

She agrees to my demand. At least her Facebook profile remains unfettered. She maintains a cheery profile picture that displays the width of her bleached smile and accentuates her pale skin. That flash does wonders for imperfections. People will encounter her online persona more often than they encounter her, so keeping a static page for the public to see will work wonders in repairing her damaged reputation.

By extension, her profile will lift mine. A few of her friends will add me. I'll snatch some social proof. When one goes up, we all do.

Thanks, I tell her. I turn to leave but she stops me.

It'll be suspicious if you come in and out like that, she tells me. Her dad will want me to stay for dinner.

I can argue this point or suck it up.

Staying in her father's good graces keeps me off the radar. Besides, I haven't eaten in a while.

Monday, January 13

Math, which has been the first class of the day all year, has been replaced by a new gym class.

No one gave me the swimming unit memo, so I ogle the half-naked bodies. The boys wear goggles and caps, so I can only tell them apart by their bodies. I'm horny. I can't wait to swim with them, even if none of them is my type. I want Hot Dad back but he left the picture and won't be returning. Robert Desmond came into my place of employment, stole my innocence and then disappeared. Good riddance.

Finding men his age range who stay in shape requires diligence. For now, my diligence needs to be focused elsewhere.

A fat kid cannonballs, splashing me. Fat kids should not be allowed to take off their clothes, not even for a swimming unit. In boys' gym class, however, the body fat becomes a talking point that keeps the other students playful, the absence of girls never dawning on them until they're sent to the locker room.

A few girls added to the class would shake up the dynamic, separate the wheat from the chaff. A few boners would result, a few fat kids would swim wearing shirts. The raging hormones would allow me to fade into the background. I wish this class had girls.

The short bald gym teacher, who I assume has had a mob career in New Jersey and is only teaching P.E. to escape his past, blows his whistle. Time to go change.

The students emerge from the pool, dripping on their way to towels. I'm sitting next to some of them. One student keeps his goggles and cap on until he's in front of me, and I wonder if there's a joke coming up.

"Can I help you?" I say, holding one towel in each hand. I see-saw them like I'm the scale of justice.

"Yeah, you can get out of here," he says. Oh, I know that accent.

Mike takes off his goggles and I shudder. Last thing I need is another threat. Death was imminent enough last time, and I feel he owes me at least one punch for that final stomach jab I gave him. I don't know what country he's from, but I assume it's a patriarchal one with emphasis placed on aggression and assertion. Perhaps being without Zack's company has reminded him of where he came from, and now he's testing his new identity on me.

Those subtle facial twitches give him away. He doesn't realize that. It's kind of cute and frightening at the same time.

"You really want me to leave? I thought we squashed our beef?"

"It's all your fault!" His voice echoes. Why does everything echo in swimming areas? Is it the chlorine? The ceiling height? Even the gymnasium doesn't echo this much.

"Easy. Relax, it's not my fault."

"I knew Eddie. It was not his fault."

"First of all, you didn't know that your friend was gay, but that's beside the point. And secondly," I sprout a second finger, "it kind of was his fault. He made that choice on his own."

"You are lying!" Now some students' attention has been averted. More eyes on me. All I need right now. The teacher turns his egg head and takes a few steps in our direction. His steps are so wimpy and unbecoming for an ex-mobster that I wonder if he's a registered therapist, walking on egg shells and searching for The Right Thing To Say.

Crap.

Mike takes off his cap, revealing a buzz cut. That shark fin nose of his must make him more fluid in the water, more aerodynamic when he runs on the tennis court.

"No, I'm not lying. Can't we just get past this?" Now I'm being the wimpy one by acquiescing. He's half-naked and I'm clothed, but he's also taller and more toned. He's standing and I'm sitting. The contrast can't be more offensive; the imbalance can't be more unfair. He still hasn't been punished for hurting me.

"No, because I won't forget what you did." His voice cracks. Raw emotion combined with brute strength does not spell a positive outcome for me. I am a lot of things, but a fighter isn't one of them.

The coach butts in with: "What's the matter?"

"Nothing is the matter," Mike says. "We are just talking." He collects himself quickly and heads to the locker room. Good, I don't have to see the hideous red splotches that were forming on his neck and upper chest. He reddens like a cartoon character.

"Youze two gonna be good tomorrow?"

"I hope so," I say.

The bell rings, reminding me that the day has barely begun.

Before I can get to second period, though, I have to visit the principal again.

ロロロ

This time, no Mrs. D. Just us guys, one on one. Mano a mano, if we are sparring.

"I've discussed this issue with Mrs. D and the superinten-dent, and ..."

Blah, blah, blah. That Bicycle playing card is still under-neath his lamp, so I can't focus on anything he's saying. I mean, one sloppy visit is acceptable, but he really should have organized his desk by now. Does he do any work on his desk?

"Are you listening to me?"

I nod, holding down my impression of a post-Depression midwife.

"As I was saying ..."

Those file cabinets are still overflowing with papers. Is it any wonder he has to be so verbose when he's addressing students? The more he says, the more grandiloquent he sounds, given his authority. Students succumb. He talks for his ego, but I won't feed it. He doesn't have a lick of knowledge pertaining to old files that have been stashed away and never sorted, discarded as the situation demands. Each new school year deserves a tabula rasa. What a pitiful administrator.

"I hope you're taking this all very seriously," he says.

"I am. Most certainly, Principal Snow."

"I'll let this issue dissolve, but ..."

Dissolve. That's what issues do. Children who are neglected have the autonomy to buck the system, become self-sufficient. Issues, however, have a life of their own. They must be acted upon, watched, studied–but they have no power without agents, the ones who create issues. He said the key phrase, which was all I wanted to hear. I agree to let the issue dissolve.

"On your end, you must not discuss this with other students."

That sounds desperate.

"Additionally, you are on a sort of probation, wherein you ..."

That sounds forced. He can't even improvise. He studies what he's going to say before he says it. That's an awful trait for a leader of four hundred and thirty-five students. He should be able to make extemporaneous decisions based on his massive gut, while still abiding by the school's code of conduct.

"I understand completely, Principal Snow."

"Good."

He stands and adjusts his tie, extending a hand toward me. I shake it without knowing what I am agreeing to. Honestly, I don't care. Humans are easy to read. He basically wants to save his reputation and look good to the superintendent, so some disciplinary action is required. He already suspended me. Now he has to intimidate me with empty threats in case I provoke the social order again. As long as I stay quiet and study hard, the entire issue will dissolve as he wants it to. Works for both of us, because I am sick of this rotten institution.

After shaking his hand, I receive a flurry of text messages from Alyssa and her friends. They all knew I'd be having a meeting with Principal Snow, probably because they were lined up outside waiting for their turn, those delinquents. Not everyone misunderstands me.

I turn my back on him and flip through the text messages, keeping my head down as I walk out. Like the obedient, docile employee high school is training me to be.

□□□

At home, I calmly throw away all junk mail and magazines, leaving the most urgent bills on the counter. Mom will appreciate that.

I don't make dinner, but I want to eat chicken pot pie. I write that down on a Post-It (Have I said how much I love Post-Its?) and place the Post-It on the freezer door. No question as to what to make for dinner, so I don't have to argue with my recovering alcoholic of a mother about what the best option for dinner might be. Mom will appreciate that.

The television remote now rests on the arm of the couch, just in case the preparation of freezer food proves too exhausting. Right there within arm's reach, no matter where on the couch one chooses to sit. Mom will appreciate that.

If the coach thinks I'm going to participate alongside an enraged lunatic, in an environment that lends itself to drowning, then he has another thing coming. I will be transferred again, before the new gym period eats me alive.

I undress and look in the mirror, proud of my progress. My muscles bulge now; a few shirts are too small now. This growth has been natural, unlike the growth of wrestlers who use too much creatine, perhaps steroids. I've been disciplined in my approach, as the fitness gurus recommend.

Scars have dissipated. My dad hit me a while ago, and there are no lasting lesions or abrasions. My skin remains supple and intact. I am well proportioned, even if my arms aren't as thick as I'd like them to be. For some reason, I want to focus on my core, to accentuate my youthfulness. I read studies about how developing the lower body staves off aging and keeps one strengthened. Hiding my age is a task far off, but I write it down anyway.

For a broke and underrated guy like me, this progress is startling. I could have easily pulled out numerous excuses as to why I couldn't work out, but I found resolutions. Socializing consumed my life. An expansive network leads to opportunities, savings, free food and guidance. Resourcefulness has kept me on track.

Unfortunately, there's no escaping the next step. Of all the possible gym classes, I fell into Michael Yulgov's. That is fine. I'll use a protractor to map a way out. The unused protractor Mrs. D put on the school supply shopping list.

I tear the tape off the plastic case and pull out the protractor. It's brand new, straight from the factory. But I still sterilize it. I unscrew the lid to Mom's vodka (which she still keeps on the night stand, as a sort of "test") and apply it to the sharp tip. I don't know how long alcohol should be left alone to sterilize, so I dump the protractor's tip in a pot of water and turn the stove on, watching the electric burner turn red.

I hold the protractor upright until the water boils. Most people don't have the attention span to watch water boil, but I do. I stand in front of the stove without checking my phone or looking out the window, waiting for that first bubble to pop. Then I set a timer for five minutes before pulling the protractor out and heading back upstairs.

In front of the mirror, with plenty of natural light, I dig the protractor's point into my forearm, carefully avoiding veins. When I was skinny, my veins seemed easier to hit, but now I have extra meat on me. Scraping a few muscles doesn't seem so scary now, even if my veins look like road blocks.

Blood trickles to the surface, forming a dark puddle that webs in all directions as I tilt my arm. I trace a line as straight as possible, careful not to go too deep. A drop of blood hits my toe. I wince, but carry on.

Repeating the process. At first, the pain caused me to squirm, but now it's euphoric. I almost want to drag the protractor multiple times, to experience what a runner has to run at least twenty minutes for. If you cut in rapid succession, you don't have time to register the pain until after you're done. Until then, there is only pleasure in the madness.

Alas, I can't have too much fun. Instead of tilting my head back and reveling in the joy of cutting, I draw red lines with surgical precision. Each cut draws more blood than the last.

Not one drop has hit the floor. I am proud of myself.

After a dozen jagged strokes, I apply ointment and adhesives to the wounds. The wounds don't have to look life-threatening; they just have to induce enough worry to relieve me of gym class with a Neanderthal.

Problem is, I should have done this a week ago. There was no possible way for me to know this outcome a week ago, so I'm rolling with the punches. I can adapt and react, unlike Principal Snow.

The lines will be bright red tomorrow morning, and I'd like them to be brown and healing, but what can ya do? They look more dramatic this way. A mere suggestion of suffering should be enough for a fat Italian gym teacher who probably bets on Sunday football games. He only wants the problem to go away; he doesn't really care about his students.

With my arm sufficiently bandaged, I lie in bed and stare at the ceiling, like I do every night. My own form of meditation. It's fun to consider the combinations, the permutations, all the possible outcomes. Tomorrow's possibilities are always more exciting than today's.

Tuesday, January 14

I heard a rumor that voting for the Prom King and Queen will be electronic. The school wants to be progressive and move away from the paper system we've had in the past. All this talk about progress. You'd think they were trying to forget about the suicide.

The changes pose no real threat to me. If anything, the changes improve my chances, because now the aspirants know to direct their attention toward a viral campaign. We're all playing online. We're all playing out in the open, where our secrets can spread rapidly. They can fester and form mold, leading to death. Rotten death.

So with those parameters set, I'll do my best to interact with several different cliques, avoiding any that might prove too detrimental to the reputation I've worked so hard to establish. I will dress more sharply. Styles can change depending on the group I'm schmoozing, but I must find a happy medium. Alyssa can help with wardrobe, because the fashion world is not one I want to dip into.

For today, my plan has already been set in motion. I head straight to the back, where the gymnasium is, and locate the gym teacher before class starts. He's talking on his burner, predictably, and before he turns his full attention to me, I overhear a preponderance of new slang terms. I merely blink when he looks at me with a countenance that might as well say: "Hey, Morty, can I call ya back later? Got a kid wants to talk to me. Yeah, yeah. Thursday poker at your place. Trumble! Ahright, bye now. What's up, kid?"

His gold necklace glitters as he moves forward. "How are ya today, Jude?"

"Well, not too good actually," I say.

"Somethin the matter?"

I nod meekly, trying to sulk. His eyes narrow, and his eyebrows go up in concern. He inquires further, forcing an explanation out of me. I pull my sleeve up and reveal the bright red marks on my forearm, the result of so much high school pressure. Woe is me!

"You should get that looked at," he says dumbly.

"I can't swim in this unit. I can't have them all asking questions. It's too much for me."

"You can wear a shoit," he suggests. I want to smack him. He knows I can't wear a shirt in an all-boys gym class. After a moment of silence, he breathes deeply and pats the top of his fuzzy head.

"I can have ya switched. Gawd, Jude, you gotta talk to someone about that there. You want to talk to the school counselor?"

He's completely flummoxed and doesn't know how to respond. He's grown accustomed to injuries, just not self-inflicted ones. He doesn't know where to start, but eventually he fumbles enough to say I can sit out.

Away from Mike.

His peon brain will catch on as soon as he's done feeling like a chump. Those same feelings he probably teases his friends for having. Girls, sure. But he's never seen self-inflicted wounds on a boy before. That hits him deep, man.

"We can talk more about this later. But right now, ya gotta sit out for today. I can get ya easily transferred." He says transferred like *transfoid*.

My work's done. I say thank you and saunter off, ready to relax. I could pay attention to what my teachers are saying, but if you don't celebrate small victories, you'll burn out.

□□□

Mom flips out, of course, and I have to talk for hours to

calm her down. I don't tell her the truth; she doesn't need to know the truth. I tell her that I wanted to try it once, to cope with the pressure I've been feeling lately, and that I'll never, ever do it again.

Around bedtime is when she decides to lay off. I mean, the situation is dire, considering the phone call she received from school about it. It was the school's fault. They shouldn't have suspended me for no good reason.

The next day we have a long talk, Mom and I, and the school therapist makes a few suggestions of her own. Some awful events must lie in the therapist's past for her to end up at this high school. High student loans, an abusive ex-boyfriend who left her with low self-esteem. She suggests that I seek therapy with her.

Mom jumps on that bandwagon immediately, much to my chagrin. Apparently I don't have health insurance coverage, so Mom can't afford to send me to an actual therapist. In addition to lack of practice, I now have another reason to avoid joining any sports teams this year. Athletics are anathema to me until I receive basic coverage, which won't be for a long time. What chance do I have of passing the try-outs? Let's face it: I haven't been training.

Everyone needs therapy, though. I'm kind of bummed. Even the school therapist needs therapy. If she had received therapy while she was in college, then she wouldn't have become a therapist. Now she's relegated to a fluffy career, one that can't be taken seriously, even if it must take seriously the patients it attracts. How shameful. She should go cut herself.

The three of us agree, right here in the school therapist's office. I will see her once a week until I am deemed stable enough to wander the halls unsupervised.

ooo

The therapist doesn't know how to read people, because she's far too nice and most likely gives every student that treatment. I wonder if she'll change her tone once I rattle off my accomplishments for the year. Unless I threaten to hurt someone—or myself—she has to keep our sessions confidential.

But why give her the chance? She doesn't need to know anything about me. I will feed her the story that most appropriately fits my wrist-cutting, and remain on the side of recovery. That means no negativity or self-doubt, only positive thoughts. As fun as this might become, I need to stay off the radar and work harder on my studies for a month or two.

Her office has two chairs on my side of the desk, and the walls seem to close in. Stepping into the hallway at the end of our session gives me freedom of movement. Fresher air and light. No windows in that dingy office.

Walking among students in the hallway doesn't feel much better, mainly because I hate them all. (Otherwise I wouldn't have alienated so many people.)

I spot Misty, who is surrounded by three Asians. Two of them are Chinese, and the third is Thai. That same guy, Pit or whoever. I suppress the urge to tell those Asians that they aren't Japanese. If Misty actually knew any Japanese people, she'd be hanging out with them instead.

She gives cash to Pit, and they both smile. Maybe she's cheating and turning into a sex pig, just like all the other Farang, the sexpats who visit Thailand for the most lustful of hedonism.

I couldn't care less about what Misty does anymore. She already outed me to the school, and that didn't hurt my reputation, so now she can't possibly hurt me. Physically she can, if she asks Clint to clobber me. For all I know, they could have broken up by now.

My business now lies in doing homework. Colleges care more about junior year grades, but I will bring up my GPA because I told myself that I could, if I really wanted to. And I will.

Thursday, January 30

These days I'm taking the bus home more often, because Eddie's dead as hell and can't pick me up. Alyssa would have her driver do it but she doesn't pay him; her dad does. Plus, I'm out of the way for her, and in the morning rush to beat the school bell, she's stressed for time enough on her own. Must be all that makeup.

I step off the bus, which doesn't pull into my driveway, and walk the extra steps through the blustering cold. Snow doesn't look as glamorous on our dirt-patched lawn. Touching the brass door handle causes me to shiver.

Inside, the temperature isn't much better. Mom has gone draconian about energy consumption, as she does every winter. Can't leave lights on even if I step away for less than one minute. Can't turn the heat up over sixty-three. Can't take hot showers; lukewarm showers are just as powerful, and the colder water encourages you to get out.

Least she could do is get a job if she wants to spout these limitations. Where the hell is she taking the car every day while I'm at school?

I walk to the back, toward the kitchen, announcing my arrival. She's clipping coupons on the kitchen table, using colorful scissors that belong in a preschool construction paper assignment. Can't afford proper kitchen shears, she'd say if I pressed her. Can't you see that I'm clipping coupons?

"Hi, Mom."

We exchange glances. Her stringy hair looks unwashed, and the bags under her eyes are as dark as her pupils. Back to old habits?

"Hi, Judie."

"What's up? You look stressed."

She sets the scissors down and folds her hands in front of her mouth, all while tapping her foot rapidly on the linoleum floor. She closes her eyes, crinkling up some crow's feet, and inhales deeply like she wants to cry. Oh, great.

"Your father, sweetie. It's your father."

"What'd he do this time?"

Mom likes to blame everyone but herself, and my dad seems to receive more blame than anybody else. For the late alimony and child support payments, she's right to blame him, but she's also the mother who cried wolf. The financial strain she won't shut up about bothers me less than she wants it to, and that is her own fault. I've heard enough of the complaints growing up. Enough.

"It's what he's not doing," she says.

"So are you going to get a job?"

"No," she says, wiping her nose. "He owes money and he's going to pay it."

"The burden is all on him?"

"What are you talking about?" She stands up. Her robe comes undone but she's still covered, thank God. "I take care of you every day. He's never here to take care of you."

"That's because you have a restraining order against him," I say calmly.

We argue family dynamics and responsibilities for well over fifteen minutes, yelling the whole time. Messing with her when I know she's relapsed gives me the edge, the trump card that I can pull out whenever I want. I won't exercise it until I'm in a pinch. Right now I don't need any such leverage to win an argument.

"I have to do my homework. Some of us take responsibility for our actions."

She has nothing to say to that. I stomp up the stairs and slam the bedroom door, which rattles the walls. A few seconds later, Mom sobs, and those gentle sobs turn into more waterworks.

That was almost too easy. I can't help myself.

Wednesday, February 12

Weeks of talking to the school therapist. I want to pull my hair out and possibly kill someone. The whole point of therapy is to pick at wounds, I've surmised. My self-inflicted cuts are less painful than the wounds therapists want you to believe you have. Anything to prescribe medication, anything. After taking enough pills, I'll either be like Mom, or locked up in an institution less forgiving than high school.

I'd rather have taken my chances in the previous gym class. Mike unleashing his aggression on me might not be so bad. It'd toughen me up.

The mind games I'm forced to play with this therapist, however, drain me. I've created too many lies and stories and they're all falling under their own weight. Nothing inherently wrong with that, but a therapist is too eager to listen. Too much confinement and confidentiality keeps the fun from spreading, and now my creativity has become stifled.

To make matters worse, the new gym class is co-ed. Co-ed sounded good at first, but the shrill laughter and physical inferiority of girls annoys me, now that I'm experiencing it. Too many girls and not enough half-naked boys. I don't even like boys my age, but they are better than girls. I can say that for myself, unlike most people who refuse to cross boundaries, because I've had sex with girls and boys. So many people claim to be on one side without having tried the other. Baffling.

Once again, a girl is hammering her nonsense into me. This therapist will be the last one I allow to do so. At least Alyssa knows who she is. She might be the only one who does.

Everyone else pretends.

This mousy therapist remains so respectful of my feelings that I want to gag right in front of her. Lashing out doesn't change her expression one bit. I've tried.

The school has mandated one more therapy session, because I seem to be making "promising progress," according to the therapist. I'll show her progress.

I'll tell her everything. The truth. I won't tell her the whole truth–just enough to whet her appetite during our final session. She'll consider me the most interesting student she's seen all year, and she won't be able to see me again. With any luck, she'll tell her girlfriends from the psychology department about my behavior. If they spend one second gabbing about me after work hours, then I will have won.

Monday, February 17

"How's the college process going?" The therapist automatically assumes that I'm going to college, like it's the default thing for a high school student to do. As if there's nothing better for an energetic eighteen-year-old to do than sit in more classes, because apparently twelve years of sitting in classes is not enough.

"Good," I say.

"You applied for financial aid already?"

"The FAFSA deadline was the fifteenth. That date has passed. What does it matter if I applied or not? I can't get more money at this point."

"Jude, that negativity is slipping in again. Did you hear it just then? It's more than just words, it's in your tone. We're trying to–"

"You've had plenty of time to cure me, but you haven't, Doctor." I lean back in the chair and relax my shoulders. My legs are spread wide open and my arms rest comfortably on the arm rests.

She jots a few notes down before looking up at me. Her glasses slip too far down her nose; she pushes them up and wiggles her nose as if she just inhaled pepper.

A long silence follows, during which I assume she's contemplating the course of our sessions. Missed notes? Improper analyses? Too little time?

"This aggression of yours–where's it coming from?" Not perky, but polite.

"It's how I was born," I say without blinking.

"I don't believe that."

Before she can recite her Psych 101 nature vs nurture crap in my presence, I elaborate. "My aggression started as a little tiny seed, and it bloomed from there. Most children, they develop personalities at a very young age. Two years old, something like that?"

She nods.

"Well, I was no different. I grew differently, that's all."

"Yes, we've talked about your rough childhood and home life. These negative thoughts become patterns that perpetuate themselves because you give them power. The way you view things–"

"Cut the bullshit."

"Excuse me, but we will avoid using language like that in this room."

"My language is unsavory? I think you like it plenty. Short dirty blond hair. Rimless glasses. Tight lips. A vertical-striped blouse. Stockings that are too dark and clash with your black skirt. And, may I say, tiny breasts. Either you're a lesbian feminist or you're attracted to men who dominate."

I lean forward. She gulps, stunned into silence.

"You like having the illusion of power. The school system bestows you with a certain authority over students, and you engage them as if you are superior. You're not. Look, I can see your lip just twitched. You know it's true."

"That's not true," she says. For the first time in our professional relationship, I catch her glimpsing at the clock.

"Yes, it is. So why don't you tell me who the man was?"

"I beg your pardon?"

"The evil man who turned you into a man-hater. The one you tried so hard to psychoanalyze and fix. He must have yelled a lot. Did he hit you too? Was he lazy?"

"This is inappropriate and irrelevant to our discussion about college."

"He was that bad, huh?"

"Our final session is finished. You may head to your next class now."

I slap my knee and laugh. Her suggestion satisfies me.

"Well then," I say. "See ya."

Studying for my next class beats staying in a stuffy room with a Lifetime movie-watching bitch. Acing tests now seems within the realm of possibility without mandatory therapy sessions competing for my time.

I knock over a garbage can on my way to Study Hall. The janitor might've seen me. I don't care.

Thursday, March 27

Colleges process applications quickly these days. They're eager to take your money. I received my acceptance letter to U of M. An unimpressive state school, but then again, my grades look terrible. Mom's happy that I don't have to attend community college. Community college wouldn't bother me.

Next step is to have her co-sign the student loan documents. No idea where that money is coming from, or how I'll survive the four years financially. I'll have to take a part-time job on campus and cross my fingers that everything works out.

Just kidding. Someone will give me the money when I ask for it. After all, Misty fell for me and paid for my gym membership. So did Eddie. College should be full of targets, and it has better access to authority figures who can actually help me.

So many opportunities. No one has to know where I'm from. I can edit my profile pages so it's harder to find my personal data. It's not quite moving away with a new identity, but close.

High school is for chumps. The big leagues are in college and beyond. When people finally treat you like you're an adult. Of course, I can refrain from matriculation and still be considered an adult, but what good is college if it can't shelter the vulnerable students from the big bad world just outside the bubble?

The possibilities excite me. Winning Prom King doesn't excite me much anymore. I won't win, not without being an athlete. That's how it goes.

Lacrosse tryouts are coming up, and I'm not participating. Call me a quitter. The papers from my last physical can't be found, and Mom can't afford to pay any more fees. Those are reasonable excuses.

At least I look like an athlete now. A major body transformation like mine deserves praise. Not that I'd show anyone, but I've logged my progress with photographs–one taken at the first of each month since starting. Photos prevent delusions, because your body can change so subtly that you hardly notice, all because you look in the mirror every day and see the same body.

I'm no fool. Those photos mean something. Those who attempt a physical overhaul without monitoring progress along the way will inevitably fail. They don't respect themselves, and maybe they are afraid of actually succeeding. Adapting to new clothing, avoiding the fatty favorites, eating at certain times, dealing with peer pressure.

Those problems are all self-imposed. Whenever a mental block rears its ugly head, I imagine an invisible alien watching me, laughing at how frail humans can be. Like, really? Humans have problems with self-discipline? Humans can't be efficient? Humans fail to achieve goals? Humans have dreams?

Identify, follow through, analyze, repeat. A simple process that works, no matter what you're trying to achieve. My problem in trying to become Prom King is that I waited until twelfth grade. It should have been my goal in middle school.

Navigating the social landscape is tricky business, and there's no telling how the electronic votes will tally out even if I do everything right. Simpler goals keep me grounded, and I'm glad to have gained a few pounds of muscle from this nasty experiment.

Or maybe I'm shooting myself in the foot. There's still time to win votes. Plenty of nappy-haired black girls remain undecided, because who are they going to vote for, a black guy? Those undecided voters really add up.

I may still have a chance. Despite my lack of athleticism, I can still attend athletic functions. My face needs to be out there as much as possible.

Friday, April 11

Alyssa and I have had sex a few more times, but I'm not complaining. She tries not to moan. I close my eyes. The rest comes easily enough, because it's casual, not serious. When she looks at me afterward, we both sigh our troubles away and try to forget what happened.

That's our arrangement, which makes me a manwhore, kind of. The sex never thrills me like it does her, but I am paid and given rides to school, a gym membership, free dinners. Her father still thinks I would never sleep with his daughter, and so I'm convinced that he is retarded. He can't smell his daughter's cooch juice at the dinner table?

Lately, however, Alyssa hasn't been keeping tabs on me. A fair selection of boys keeps her interest more than past flings. She's told me that I can't cramp her style.

Taking note of all the boys who wander in and out of her bedroom can drain anyone's morale. Instead, I keep her within reach, sending a text message once every four days, keeping the rhythm consistent but not pushy.

In the mean-time, studying takes precedence. I still have to graduate.

Out of left field, I receive a text message from Zack, asking if I want to meet him for lunch tomorrow. Although we're still friends on Facebook, I haven't spoken to him since Halloween.

Saturday, April 12

We meet at a trailer that sells food–a diner.

Zack Eldin's waiting at the front door with Alyssa Zaianassey by his side, and I can't quite believe it. I thought he was done with her, but maybe I was wrong. It's so like him to change his mind. He doesn't know what he wants, so he goes around sticking his penis into every hole until he finds one that doesn't whine too much afterward.

He gestures, with a curled finger, to come forward, and I cross the gravel parking lot. Weeds cover the diner's exterior.

The sound of gravel crunching beneath tires. An engine humming. I hear it coming from behind the diner. As I approach the steps leading to the front door, I spot a black Mercedes pull out from the back and onto the main road. Either Alyssa is going home with Zack, or her driver wants to wait elsewhere.

Zack pats me on the shoulder and ushers me inside, holding the door open so that I may enter first, before Alyssa. A waitress greets us without a smile and mimes what she wants to say instead of speaking aloud, because apparently customers are supposed to read lips.

"Four," Zack says.

"This way," the waitress says after grabbing four laminated menus.

A delicate hand finds its way to my shoulder. "Connor's coming too," Alyssa says.

We're led to a window booth near the back. The plastic seat has been ripped, revealing the yellow stuffing that's been padding people's rumps for God knows how long. Some people liken diners to charm; I liken them to filth. The stained silverware rests on the bare table, no napkin underneath.

I slide into the booth so that I'm facing Zack.

"Whose choice was this?" I say.

"Mine," Zack says. "All mine."

The fifty-year old waitress flips her pad open and asks if she can bring us any beverages.

"Do you have water?" I say.

"Uh-huh," she grunts, torturing me with her cigarette breath.

"That's tap water?"

"Comes out of the tap, yes."

"Can I have bottled water instead?"

"We only serve tap water here."

"You know what? I just won't have anything to drink." I smile ironically and lean back, prompting the other two to speak up. "Guys, you want anything to drink at this wonderful establishment?"

"Tea," Alyssa says, startled. "Black. No sugar."

"Coke," Zack says.

The waitress indifferently jots those down and waddles away to fetch their drinks.

"Now she's gonna spit in our food," Zack says.

Alyssa strokes his bare arm. "No, she won't."

"Do you see anyone else at this diner?" I point to the empty booths everywhere. "It's lunchtime on a Saturday, and it's not busy. She probably spits in everyone's food."

Zack opens his mouth, but the front door opens before he says anything. A ringing bell prompts the three of us to look in that direction. It looks like Connor Welbach, but he has considerably less hair. He must have buzzed it all away with clippers. Additionally, a pair of black aviator sunglasses overtakes a large portion of his face. He walks toward us, and with each step, I am more and more sure that he is, in fact, Connor. The scar on his forehead has healed, but it's noticeable. So is the limp.

"Hey!" Alyssa squeals.

"Sup, my man? How are you?" Zack can't stand, because Alyssa's blocking him in. If she weren't, I'm certain he would stand and then they'd do a super-secret handshake before bumping chests.

Connor merely grins and sits next to me. The booth deflates under his heft, and I pop up. My knee hits the table.

Alyssa clears her throat first and picks up the menu. The others follow suit, and then so do I. With my peripheral vision, I notice that Connor has not removed his sunglasses. He must be too cool for us. Surprisingly, neither Alyssa nor Zack comments on them. The sunglasses are simply a part of Connor, as if, at birth, he squirted out of his mother's vagina wearing them.

The waitress, whatever her name is, returns with a white tea cup filled to the top with black tea. When I say filled to the top, I mean that I don't understand how she managed not to spill a single drop. In her other hand, Zack's Coke, although his glass is not filled to the top.

The waitress notices Connor and perks up. If she looked like a female Quasimoto before, then she looks like a WASP dressed in waitress garb now. Her eyes soften and her speech improves in both pronunciation and eloquence.

"And what can I get for you, young man?" She sets the two drinks down and then turns her whole body toward Connor. With one hand resting on the back of his seat, she looks like she might lean forward, pushing her flabby breasts in his face.

Connor answers, "I'll have a water."

"Anything for you, darling."

The waitress puckers her blood red lips and then fetches Connor's water. No wonder the place is empty during a Saturday lunch hour–it's fucking weird here. Instead of acknowledging me, Connor has the gall to ask Zack what we've been talking about. Zack fills him in, saying that I thought the waitress might spit in our food.

"I don't think she will," Connor says to me. "I really don't think she will."

I ignore him and turn to Zack. "Coming here was really your idea?"

"Yes," Alyssa chimes in. "It most certainly was."

"Why?"

"Just because," Zack says. He shrugs like he doesn't care. Like we could've either come here or McDonald's, but that it doesn't make a difference either way.

They barely glance at their menus. I guess they knew what they wanted before they invited me. I still don't know what I want.

"How are we paying for this? I don't have a lot of money if we're splitting."

"I'll pay," Alyssa says.

"Okay."

The waitress returns with an iced mug, full of water and four ice cubes. She sets it on a Hard Rock Cafe coaster. No one else gets a coaster.

I should have ordered water.

"What can I get you all today?"

"I want your steak breakfast sandwich on an English muffin," I say. If Alyssa's paying, then I'm ordering whatever I want. "Please double toast the English muffin. I'd also like two sides of hash browns with some peanut butter, a cup of your fruit salad. Oh right, and I'd also like two crispy strips of bacon on the side, so I can add them to my breakfast sandwich."

The waitress writes this down quickly. Her tongue is sticking out as she concentrates on her writing, and her lips are slightly curled upward. Maybe she enjoys the challenge of capturing a big delivery.

"Are you sure you wouldn't like anything to drink?"

I glance at Connor's iced mug of water and tell her I want that. Her face sinks and she goes from looking like an upper middle class WASP to a frumpy, arthritic coffee bitch. Regardless, she writes down what I asked for, I think.

At this point, I'm convinced she's going to spit in my food. Might as well order the water to wash it down.

Zack, Alyssa and Connor place their orders too, but I don't pay attention to what they're getting. Once finished, the waitress walks away, leaving behind the faint scent of nicotine.

"Why did you invite me here today?" I blurt.

Zack's eyes widen with interest. Alyssa looks taken aback by my question. They both glance at each other and adopt neutral expressions before Zack answers.

"I think you know why."

"Enlighten me."

"We're here to catch up."

"In what way?"

"For starters, Alyssa's my girlfriend now. That means you can't have her. No more hanging out. No more free rides. And after today, no more free lunches. I understand that you had sex a few times. That's off limits too." Zack takes a sip of his Coke and I can almost see the fizz hitting his nose. He wipes his mouth before continuing. "Obviously, that means she's going to Prom with me this year. You'll have to find someone else."

He pulls a few strands of blond hair from his eyes and takes another sip, indicating that he's finished. Alyssa clutches his arm like the backstabbing slut she is.

"And I just wanted to say, Jude, that I forgive you," Connor says, suddenly.

"Forgive me for what?" My heart rate quickens. I can barely breathe in this cramped space. The smeared window beside me allows no access to fresh air. It can't open.

"I forgive you," Connor repeats. His tone sounds sincere, but I can't see past the sunglasses to be sure. "I forgive you, Jude. I forgive you for everything."

I grab a butter knife and squeeze the handle until my knuckles turn white. At this very second, more than anything in the world, I have the overwhelming urge to stab Connor in the femoral artery. Then we'll see how forgiving he can be. My breathing quickens. My cheeks redden.

Alyssa decides to open her big mouth to speak, and she never speaks as well as she sucks dick. "Think of this as a going-away lunch. We're all willing to move on from our issues, to leave them in the past. We're all going to college this fall, so there's no point in being angry at each other."

A few weeks ago she wanted to have angry sex. She slapped

me repeatedly until I got angry, and then she kicked me in the balls really, really hard. I cringed and fell to the floor and had every right to bludgeon her to death with her Buddha statue, but she sat on my face before I knew what was happening.

And then we had angry sex.

I'm even angrier now–and a lot less horny. I just want to drag her to the kitchen by her hair and then dump boiling water all over her flawless half-Caucasian, half-Singaporean skin. For believing she can dismiss me so easily, she deserves that much.

"This is the best thing for all of us," Zack says. Decapitation would be best for him, right after a fast castration.

I honest-to-God want to scream. The waitress returns with our food. That relieves some of the tension. I don't inspect my sandwich for spit or grime because I don't care anymore. The food stopped me from doing something that would land me in prison.

"I think you're right," I say. "After today, I think it's best if we don't see each other again."

Outside, the trees stand leafless. Power lines droop between electricity poles. Ground with gravel and pavement but no grass. Skies without blue. I expect it to rain, but it won't. The weather man said so. The dark skies will hover above us, teasing us and taunting us, and there's nothing we can do about it. We just tread carefully, moving along day by day.

Connor removes his aviators but doesn't look at me. "Best for all of us."

He and Kristen McNicky might have broken up. I don't know. Whatever happens today, tomorrow can be better. This table wants nothing to do with me. That is fine. I don't need them.

Friday, May 2

I haven't cast my vote for Prom King or Queen this year. Since I learned that the school wants to try a digital voting system, I've lost some interest in the event. Now, anyone can log on from any computer and cast a vote. No paper counters needed. Some things should never go digital.

Keeping up with the trends has been difficult, and I'm almost certain that I won't win. I've burned enough bridges to merit a careless approach to the ending school year.

Mike's match isn't going too well for him. There are maybe seventeen spectators outside, on the bleachers, quietly watching. Lacrosse and football have noisier crowds that can encourage the teams, but here we have to watch our players win or lose with muted expressions.

The sport's elegance is killing me, and I want nothing more than to shout at Mike as he's preparing to lob. I'm sitting in the front row, wearing bright red so he can see me. When he changes court, he might imagine my eyes on his back, and perhaps fumble a few advantages to the opponent's deuces. I can only hope.

Now, in early May, the trees still haven't regained all their leaves, but not a single person in the audience has commented on the weather. The sun blinds half the players at a time.

Deuce. Mike's about to lose the set. Once his will is crushed, he'll decline further until he reaches an inevitable loss that I'd like to give myself credit for. It's what he deserves for hitting me in the hallway, and I'll attend every match to remind him of that mistake if I have to. If he wins, then I'll quell his loutish behavior with a backhanded congratulations that I'm sure will flare his temper, hampering the rest of his day, the positive inertia sliding into regret, admonishment and hatred.

Zack, Connor and Alyssa have told me to stay away from them only. Not that I'll listen, because they don't have control over me. I will attend every school function until graduation, and once that sinks in, they'll be avoiding me. They have no leverage. They are not even my equals.

Advantage to opponent. Mike's not going to win, I can feel it.

Zack and Alyssa are such idiots, hooking up so close to the end. Alyssa said it herself: we're all going to college in the fall. They'll break up over the summer, whether they attend the same college or not, and memories of each other's genitalia will be the only take-away gift as they approach adulthood. True high school sweethearts–the ones who last decades together–are a myth.

Set. Michael Yulgov loses the set.

Change courts. Michael faces away from me and toward the budding trees.

Even better revenge would be to take Connor's sloppy seconds. Kristen has become a train wreck right before our eyes. The Help Kristen McNicky Get Cheechy Foundation has been funded entirely by Alyssa Zaianassey. Connor Welbach should know that. Kristen should have told him that. I'm sure they were both too embarrassed to talk about it, so the easiest solution was to break up.

Now that Mike's facing away from me, I don't have to scowl so much. I whip out my phone to ask Kristen when we can hang out.

Whenever you want, she replies. Just bring a bag.

Sunday, May 4

To avoid buying another bag at the public library, I tell Kristen that I can only meet her at church.

Once we see each other, it's as if no time has passed.

Before, we bonded over religion; now, we bond over our willingness to escape it. This happened gradually at first, but after introducing her to weed, she quickly adopted the right attitude going forward.

Her clothes are more muted, less colorful. There aren't any frills or doilies or other embellishments you might find on a flower bearer's dress, as before. Now: grey jeans and a black shirt. She could've taken the time to apply makeup more evenly, instead of applying so much eye shadow. That comes with the slutty burnout territory.

After suffering through another sermon by the hypocrite up front, Kristen and I head outside to have a catching-up chat.

"So you didn't bring any?"

"No," I say. "This is church. Have a little bit of respect."

"Fuck."

"Hey."

"Sorry, Jesus."

A few well-dressed families pass us and head to their SUVs. We're standing right next to the door, but we don't hold the door open for anyone. Most of these people can probably afford high-end family portraits.

"Good stuff, good stuff. So here's a thought," I say. "Want to be my prom date?"

Kristen stares at me as if I'm joking. Despite her downward spiral, there's a part of her that truly believes she's one of the cool girls, because I haven't plucked her away from feminine form entirely. Her friends have changed, but she's still one of the girls, and she'll carry her righteous reputation with her always.

"You know, as a joke. Everyone knows the whole prom thing is lame anyways."

"Well, I dunno," she stammers.

"You liked that stuff I gave you last time, right? I can get that again, it's just that the guy's out of town. Trust me when I say he's willing to work with me."

She bites my line, and now it's time to reel her in.

"Really, I try this stuff every time before I give it to you. But pretty soon I'll have to start charging. Just saying. Can't have it free forever. Anyway, going to Prom with me is only a minor chore. A few hours and it's over. When my dealer gets back from Colorado next month, we'll have a Mary Jane summer and–"

"Fine, I'm in."

Mr. McNicky exits from the front entrance and walks over to us while his wife bids farewell to her once-a-week zombie friends. Kristen's dad remains ignorant and hasn't caught on to his daughter's behavior save for a newly acquired wardrobe. It's like he's never taken a puff before.

"Jude!" he says.

"Hey, Mr. McNicky!"

We shake hands and do a little hug. So glad I came dressed up today. Someone has to be a positive influence on his daughter if her secular friends at school won't. A few lies about college plans tells Mr. McNicky that I'm motivated, and simply being here tells him that I have a bright future with the Lord. Oh ye who are easily deceived! By someone who only had to show up and smile.

"Dad, is it all right if Jude takes me to Prom?"

"Honey, after what that Connor boy did to you, letting Jude take you's like a gift from God." He chuckles and actually holds his belly, then looks at me. "Son, you have my blessing."

"Blessing for what, may I ask?" Mrs. McNicky appears and rests a hand on her husband's shoulder. "What's going on?"

Kristen perks up. "Jude's going to take me to Prom."

Mrs. McNicky shoulders her purse and embraces me with her skeleton. Her perfume assaults my sense of smell, but I return the embrace nonetheless. Her wire bra pokes me hard, and I wonder how she and Mr. McNicky have sex without serious injury. He is too fat and might crush her; her scent can give rash or lesion.

Mrs. McNicky says, "I can't wait to go shopping."

Saturday, May 24

At Alyssa's place, the senior class meets for Prom pictures. Her father's idea, so he can show off his family's opulence. If you got it, flaunt it.

On this sunny May day, we pose for group pictures in the budding garden. Full bloom won't be for a few more weeks, but the verdure lures everyone in. For those who are afraid of bees, the stone deck offers a cool place to stand, elevated above the rest.

All maids are on staff today, and they're dressed in white uniform. Some Filipina, some Chinese. I don't think anyone notices or cares except for the Zaianassey family. Despite their interracial family tree, they seem to love exercising dominance over other Asian breeds.

Kristen and I are coordinating with purple, to demonstrate our school spirit. My purple tie makes me look gayer than normal. If people don't like that, then too bad.

Connor Welbach is talking to his new girlfriend's parents by the fountain, and I have half a mind to interrupt them, but Kristen grabs my arm and pulls me to her. She's deluded if she thinks I would actually fight for her. I just want to renege on my word to Connor, Zack and Alyssa, because I can.

On the other hand, they carry on as if I don't exist, as if there's no way I can spoil their special day. The arrogance angers me, but only because they're not frustrated. They smile and they laugh.

I drag my date inside and snatch a wine glass, telling a Filipina to pour me some red. She knows who I am and the only resistance is an index finger in front of her lips. *Shhhh.*

Kristen groans and frantically turns her head to see if anyone noticed. She shrugs and concludes that we're in the clear, and so she sneaks a few sips. Judging by her puckered lips and narrowed eyes, she's not fond of the taste.

The sight of everyone smiling in one spot makes me want to throw up. Their faces disgust me. I've seen these faces morph over the years into the oily, pimply veneers of today. Less comedogenic makeup and more benzyl peroxide would be a great start. Kristen, however, has applied her makeup with moderate strokes and in the right places, so I don't look like a tool standing next to her. I told her that she had to apply it properly, or else she couldn't be seen next to me, and thus, no hash. Now that's what I call foresight.

Enough of the chatter. Once the garden has become an overused backdrop, the kids and parents make their way inside, to the foyer. The parents are getting ready to leave their children to have a lasting high school memory, and the kids are trying too hard to kick them out.

One parent steps forward and makes an announcement on behalf of all parents: Use condoms if you decide to do anything. Now, in their day, a tidbit like that probably would not have gone over too well with the authority, but not one parent in the audience blinked. Perhaps they've all given up on controlling their kids, as they should have.

I'm the only one whose parents have not shown up, and I want to break free of my shackles more than anyone. I give my own little speech without even clearing my throat. Assuming the center of the foyer enables me to command everyone's attention.

"I just wanted to say that this has been a tough year at our school, and even though we've all had a hard time dealing with loss, we are able to recover as a community. I'm talking about Eddie, of course. He was my boyfriend, and I've been hit especially hard by all this. As much as we'd like to think we knew him, I guess we didn't, at least not very well. He's been on my mind every day, and sometimes it makes sleeping difficult, because I can't stop crying. I can't help but wonder if any of it was my fault. I feel like I could have done more. More of what? I don't know. It pains me to think about it, but I can't stop."

A quick glance at the crowd reveals angry faces behind agreeable, sympathetic ones. The angry ones are the usual suspects, those Negative Nelsons: Clint, Zack, Mike and Company. Boo hoo. They can shut up and let me continue. I paid more attention to Eddie than anyone, and if they knew that, then they wouldn't be so angry all the time. After all, their failure to understand Eddie resulted in his death.

"But tonight, I want Prom to be in honor of Eddie Fischer, who made us all laugh; who encouraged us to do our best; whose brilliance made us reexamine ourselves."

My speech garners loud applause that echoes throughout the expansive foyer. Facial expressions run the full spectrum, from tearful to tickled. A few of my fellow classmates aren't clapping, but they're just haters. That kind of negativity won't take them far.

Misty clutches Clint's arm and he pulls her close, as if protecting her from me. Well, I don't care. I've upgraded from Misty to Kristen, who's now yanking my arm in approval.

"You liked that little speech?"

"Of course," Kristen says. "I've never seen that side of you."

"Well, I'm trying. There's a lot more of me to see, if you play your cards right."

Wearing the purple tie allowed me to finish that speech. School spirit grants me the right to exploit everyone's desire for a peaceful future, skewing the results in my favor.

Reaction

Stepping out of the limo brings focus. Being stuck in that cramped space with a bunch of teenagers who tilted their knees away from me does not spell happy vibes. Regardless, I will remain positive. They can be petty if they want.

Prom night in the school gymnasium feels wrong. We've had so many school assemblies this year, I can't help but think another tragedy's just minutes away.

Kristen's walking arm in arm with me, wowing lookers-on with her purple dress. We are the Royal Ocelots tonight, no doubt. She's regaining some of her popularity, but maybe not enough to win.

Now that I've been seen with her, I can stray for a bit. The side table has an assortment of crackers and cheeses. Flanking the food, punch bowls on either side. I've never seen purple fruit punch before; somehow the school found enough in its budget to find grape-flavored water. I spit in one of the bowls.

"Jude, do you like this song?" Kristen yells in my ear. There are strobe lights, streamers and speakers everywhere. Also in the school budget. Wow, you'd think the school would hire better teachers.

"No, it's lame."

"Cheer up. Here, dance with me."

She takes my hand and leads me to the dance floor, where I stumble a few times before achieving a natural rhythm. I play the role of an affable male prom date, whose goal is to satisfy his demanding princess. If she's having more fun than I, then she secured the better deal, because I will still have to buy the

224 · Thad Lomer

weed (unless I convince her otherwise).

During a slow song, I hold Kristen close and spy over her shoulder. My main aggressors–those who used to be my allies–don't seem to notice that I'm here, adopting this quacky live-and-let-live attitude, all because of this stupid American tradition.

Even Principal Snow has fallen for it. He seems to be deep in conversation with Mr. K and a few others. Perhaps discussing their summer plans to take cruises and fuck barely legal girls who remind them of the hot students of their classes, the indiscreet ones who live too close to home.

"Jude," Kristen says, looking up from my chest. "I'm so glad I met you."

"Yeah, yeah. Me too. Now be quiet."

"What?"

"I like this song."

"Oh."

Far away, over by the food (of course), Clint's holding hands with a Chinese chick. I immediately scan the room for Misty, and she's a few yards away, holding hands with Pit. They can't possibly be secure enough in their relationship to swap dates tonight; I don't care how many Hagen-Dazses they've shared in the privacy of their own homes.

□□□

After twenty more minutes of slow dancing, Principal Snow takes the microphone, preparing us for the Prom King and Queen reveal.

Finally.

A spotlight focuses on the wall, where he stands beneath purple and white banners. The school mascot, our wretched Ocelot, shakes and wiggles beside him, and I'm wondering who would be moronic enough to dance like that, because it's not Zack's sister.

"And now, after a long and eventful school year ..."

Blah. He starts every announcement the same way. I tune

him out and observe the attentive faces surrounding me, and they remind me of churchgoers.

Kristen squeezes my arm, as if prompting visible excitement.

"And in light of this year's tragedy, I would like us all to take a moment of silence to remember ..."

Fireflies have no time to waste on commemorative gestures. They're too busy building a habitat, hoping a construction crew doesn't lay pavement. Fireflies didn't exist in the Cambrian period, I don't think. They made the season finale's romance look smarmy, not just because of historical inaccuracy, but because they were animated with CGI. Fireflies are endangered, that's their excuse.

"Without further ado, I'd like to formally announce this year's Prom Queen. Even I don't know who it is, folks. Let's see here." He rubs his bald head. "Oh! This year's Prom Queen is ..."

Everyone leans forward, including me.

"The one and only Misty!"

The world must be coming to an end. Everyone in attendance is clapping, even if some of the popular kids groaned at first. Kristen is clapping, cheering her on. The applause is wild and unconditional and senseless. I've worked too hard to reach this result. Misty's wearing the ugliest Prom Queen tiara I've ever seen—and it's still too beautiful for her frizzy, nappy hair. If you only had your sense of touch to go by, you might assume she's black.

"And our Prom King for this year is ..."

I swear to God, if it is Clint, I will stab him myself.

"Eddie Fischer!"

Applause starts but abruptly ends once I start screaming.

The room quiets. Reproachful looks come my way. Kristen lets go of my arm and fades into the background, and other students within my immediate vicinity recede, so that I am left alone in the center of my own circle. Dramatically, the spotlight falls on me, but I can't see anyway. It is for their own good that they're out of my reach, because I could kill someone right now.

"I'm sorry?" Principal Snow says. "Is there something the matter out there?"

The crowd looks at him, then me. Him, then me. Music's stopped. All or nothing.

"Why? It's just not *right*," I shout, straining my voice, burning my throat.

"Jude, is that you making all that noise? What's the problem?"

"Eddie can't win because he can't be nominated. Eddie is dead. Dead people can't win contests. Dead people shouldn't–"

"Dude, shut the fuck up." A voice from the crowd. Possibly Michael Yulgov's, because, thanks to my obtrusive presence, he's lost a few tennis matches, and I guess this is his cowardly form of retaliation.

"Shut the fuck up."

The crowd titters and trains their hateful eyes on me. All I want is to die and take the throne away from Eddie. There should be room for a fresh new face. But no one else agrees. The chatter increases in volume.

"That's enough," Principal Snow says. "Everybody, that's enough."

The crowd approaches me in riotous unison, and I just have to smile. I feel a blow to my back. Hands cover my body, making me want to suffocate under the collective stink of sweating adolescents imprisoned by makeup, hair spray and rented outfits. But not a single blow hurts, because I've been trained to tolerate pain since I was five years old.

I laugh.

"Everybody, that is enough." Principal Snow's hollering now, so everyone stops the mob mentality. No more witch hunting, peeps.

He continues: "Jude, because you have so much to say, maybe you'd like to take this crown instead? How does that sound? Would you like to take Eddie's crown and be an utter disgrace to his memory?"

Everyone waits for my response, because the ability to take such a beating and voice my thoughts in an unshaken, loud and charismatic way emboldens my presence. They all know not to mess with me, to deny me the prize that is rightfully mine. Walking upright, I proudly approach my throne, and the entire gymnasium brims with contempt.

Finally, I won! I am the Prom King. I may be standing next to the ugliest Prom Queen in history, but who cares. They think that my behavior is pitiful just because I do not act like them, conform to their codes of conduct, speak with any humility or shame ... but the objective has been met, and that's all that matters.

That's how the world works: results matter more than execution. If one achieves perfect results using ambiguous morals, then new laws will be introduced to facilitate a production that grants benefits and compromises to those affected. But make no mistake, results matter most.

I won.

I won, and the school hates me, but I don't care, because I won.

I break the crown in half and stomp on it before the teachers boot me from the spotlight. The look on Misty's face is priceless. She is crying.

Abreaction

The rest of the evening unravels in the most pathetic way. Everyone's posturing and pretending, insisting that they're not disturbed or offended, that they can write this off as a minor outburst by a crazy person. Right, *I'm* the crazy one.

The worst part about the evening is that I'll have to call home for a ride, because although I can handle a few jabs, I can't handle being at the mercy of a sour driver whose lack of restraint is life-threatening. Fair enough.

I dial Mom's cell but no answer.

I try again but no answer.

I walk outside and wander the parking lot–caring not a lick about possibly getting mugged–and the open air gives me perfect reception. But no answer. Looking into the night sky, I recall the year's events, thinking of how I might improve next year.

An hour later, I learn that my house has burned down.

ㅁㅁㅁ

Principal Snow shuttles me home, despite our differences, because his reputation is at stake and he wants to spin tragedies to reflect well on him. Hey, that's his job. His act is convincing too, because he seems to care about the fire more than I do.

I only regret having missed it.

Turning onto our street, Principal Snow has his doubts about getting us through all the barriers and tape, but I remind him that I live here. The cops, firefighters and medics have to let me through and witness the charred remains of a property that never belonged to us. At least its remains still complement the squalid, neighboring rentals.

Our landlord is outside with his mouth agape, his hand in front of it, looking much like a caricature. It's hard not to laugh, because I know he's only thinking about insurance.

Escaping from Snow's clutches, I approach the only reliable source of information currently available: Sheriff Roswell. Snow watches from afar, perhaps aware that his usefulness has ended, and that he should go home now.

"Now son, answer me this: Do you have any enemies? Any ball busters who might want to cause you harm?"

Of all the people I've hurt, I can't think of one who might go to such extremes, but what's done is done. I shake my head in reply.

"Well, that's a damn shame. We're thinkin arson, but we'll get to the bottom of it. For your mom's sake."

"My mom?"

"Didn't you see her, son?" He looks bewildered and points to the nearest flashing ambulance. "She's being taken away as we speak."

"Oh."

"Critical condition."

"Oh, I see."

"Well, go on then. Ride the ambulance with her. I know this must be shocking to you, but you have to be strong. Ya hear?"

I nod and try to look like a wounded soldier. If only a biting cold wind would blow in my face, I might be able to shed a few tears. I'd have to keep my eyes open and reset my mental timer, but I could let out a minor sob before leaving the sheriff to his own devices.

"Are you gonna be a strong young man?"

Jesus Christ. He's more teary-eyed than I am. Considering how he sees the seedy side of human nature on a daily basis, those tears are unwarranted. I should take his job.

"Stay with your mother, Jude. Go on now." A nudge sends

me on my way. For some reason, people can't seem to keep their hands off of me. My muscle gain over the last eight months has transformed me into something irresistible.

So it looks like I won't be getting any sleep tonight, because sleeping's not allowed when your mother is hospitalized. Staying in character is an absolute imperative until my tragedy becomes third-page news. With the glut of status updates posted hourly, this mishap should be buried in no time. Take that, Eddie Fischer.

As I gently hold my mom's bandaged hand, I think about the future. About the stupid state school that accepted me; about financial aid; about where I'm going to live this summer; about the summer job I'll be forced to take. And then it hits: my mom would be better off dead, because those burns are going to make her want to kill herself anyway, and I could really use whatever life insurance money I'm owed. Fucking bitch junkie ruining my life again. If I didn't care about being locked up, I'd pull away the tubes and needles and ice packs.

Like I said, the end result matters more than the process.

As much as I'd like to end her misery, I can't afford that on my record. Despite this year's setbacks, my progress has been remarkable. I've truly grown as a person–physically, mentally, socially. If you want an enchanting future, self-discipline will take you there. If I stay focused, there's no limit to how far I can go.

The future looks promising, no doubt about that. The first semester away from this town will give me more ideas than I know what to do with.

On that note, many college freshmen have no focus and jump from major to major, lacking a clear idea of what they want to do in life, fearing that their major is permanent and that it may incorrectly define them (yet they have no problem getting tattoos).

Well, because I'm not an idiot like them, I've already given my concentration serious thought. High school has shown me what's possible when one has the right connections, and I want to expand on what I've learned thus far by majoring in political philosophy.